Museum Visits

ÉRIC CHEVILLARD

Museum
Visits

Translated from the French by
Daniel Levin Becker

Edited by Daniel Levin Becker and
Daniel Medin

A MARGELLOS
WORLD REPUBLIC OF LETTERS BOOK

Yale UNIVERSITY PRESS | NEW HAVEN & LONDON

The Margellos World Republic of Letters is dedicated to making literary works from around the globe available in English through translation. It brings to the English-speaking world the work of leading poets, novelists, essayists, philosophers, and playwrights from Europe, Latin America, Africa, Asia, and the Middle East to stimulate international discourse and creative exchange.

The texts in this volume were originally published in French by Éditions Fata Morgana in the following collections: *Scalps, Commentaire autorisé sur l'état de squelette, Péloponnèse,* and *Détartre et désinfecte;* © Éditions Fata Morgana 2004 for *Scalps,* 2007 for *Commentaire autorisé sur l'état de squelette,* 2013 for *Péloponnèse,* and 2017 for *Détartre et désinfecte.* For details see the Credits page.

The Credits page constitutes a continuation of the copyright page.

Yale University Press books may be purchased in quantity for educational, business, or promotional use. For information, please e-mail sales.press@yale.edu (U.S. office) or sales@yaleup.co.uk (U.K. office).

Set in Source Serif type by Motto Publishing Services.
Printed in the United States of America.

Library of Congress Control Number: 2023903180
ISBN 978-0-300-25411-2 (paperback : alk. paper)

A catalogue record for this book is available from the British Library.

This paper meets the requirements of ANSI/NISO Z39.48-1992 (Permanence of Paper).

10 9 8 7 6 5 4 3 2 1

Contents

Foreword

DANIEL MEDIN

The author of one of the most massive bodies of work in contemporary French letters is, at heart, a miniaturist. This may seem counterintuitive after a glance at his bibliography: Éric Chevillard has published no fewer than twenty-two novels, not to mention several books in other genres. He also wrote a weekly column on new fiction for *Le Monde*'s book pages from 2011 to 2017 and since 2007 has maintained a blog, *L'autofictif,* consisting of three entries per day; the special-edition hardcover collecting its first decade spans more than twelve hundred pages. (The five thousandth entry went live while this Foreword was being drafted.) And yet Chevillard's true genius is for the small form, which has served him as a reliable foundation for lengthier projects. The present volume gathers a representative sampling of the short-form work he has published over the years with Fata Morgana, an Occitan printing house that specializes in beautifully produced editions, often illustrated by notable visual artists.

The first challenge of introducing a collection like *Museum Visits* is deciding what to call its constituent texts. It would be misleading to refer to them as "short stories," a form with recognizable parameters in English; instead, the texts that follow often consist entirely of observations and imaginings, verbal theatrics and gags, usually at the expense of the "story" Chevillard *could* have told had he wanted to. Though they often overlap or echo, many of these pieces easily stand alone, requiring no prior contextualization. The translator and I have decided to emphasize such works, even if that has meant omitting selections from beloved Fata Morgana collections such as *Zoologiques* or *Dans la zone d'activité,* whose contents enact new variations on an overarching formal pattern or theme.

The appellation we have settled on is "short prose," a conveniently functional term that recalls a distant ancestor. I'm thinking of two of the books Kafka consented to see published during his lifetime: *Contemplation* (1913) and the unacknowledged masterpiece *A Country Doctor* (1920). The prose in these volumes, which includes celebrated works such as "In the Gallery," "Before the Law," and "A Report to an Academy," emerged directly out of a feuilleton culture that thrived during the final years of the Austro-Hungarian Empire. Kafka's texts are linguistically playful, self-reflective, and aphoristic; they are as diminutive in length as they are in their unabashedly anti-Homeric stance and spirit. ("Nothing, on reflection, is sufficient to tempt one to come first in a race"—that's the representatively unheroic first sentence of "For the Consideration of Amateur Jockeys," which appears in *Contemplation.*)[1] And yet, reading them, we encounter in crystallized form the qualities that established his posthumous reputation decades later.

At the time of their appearance, Kafka was what we now call a writer's writer: admired by influential editors and critics but largely invisible to the greater public. And though by any measure one of the most critically successful authors working in French today, Chevillard inhabits a similar paradox. His fans include such intrepid writers as Lydie Salvayre and Pierre Senges at home, Anne Weber and Rick Moody abroad. Prominent reviewers from Nelly Kaprièlian (*Les inrockuptibles*) to Raphaëlle Leyris (*Le monde des livres*) have weighed in enthusiastically about his fiction. The pithy zing of his sentences is regularly and gleefully quoted on Twitter, though Chevillard himself has never owned a mobile phone. Since 2018, Maison de la Poésie, one of Paris's best-curated venues for literary events, has hosted close to twenty installments of "Le marathon *Autofictif*"—solo readings of selections from his blog by the actor Christophe Brault—an honorific concentration bestowed on few if any of Chevillard's peers. Appreciation extends to the academy as well, where his writings are the frequent focus of scholarly books, theses, papers, and conferences.

And yet Chevillard remains anything but a household name. This is partly by design, since his fiction dispenses with storytelling's most conventional elements, beginning with plot and character. The condition is reinforced by his outsider's temperament; though genial and polite, Chevillard is ill at ease in performative settings and rarely participates in readings or festivals. And if the most glamourous French prizes have shunned his work, this is not due solely to their aesthetic conservatism or their historic bias against smaller publishing houses, even ones as storied as his longtime home, Éditions de Minuit; we must also acknowledge the memorably apt, unpardonably entertaining takedowns Chevillard has published of novels by individuals with a permanent seat on their juries. When one such celebrity author used the pretext of a book review to reproach him for being "a failure of a great writer," Chevillard riposted that same evening in *L'autofictif:* "Decidedly, we share nothing in common, as he is a triumph of a mediocre writer."[2]

Even in such an exchange, though, the qualities that distinguish Chevillard's writing from that of his contemporaries are evident: his spontaneity, his sparkling wit, his refined irony and fetching irreverence. His sentences are *animated,* like the imagination that forms them. Even his detractors concede that he is laugh-out-loud funny. A supreme absurdist, Chevillard operates like a Gallic strain of Monty Python, exploiting faulty reasoning to the point of overkill—and then continuing a few steps farther. Consider "The Soup," which chronicles the anxious cogitations of a speaker who might have neglected to shut off the burner before leaving the house. His reflections begin rationally enough, surmising that the boiling water has by now evaporated, charring the contents of the pot. But soon they are carried away—to the delighted recognition of anyone who's ever indulged in catastrophic speculation—by the devastating chain of consequences that must necessarily follow:

> Drops of ebonite will drip onto the kitchen floor, the linoleum will catch fire, the flames will start to spread everywhere, making themselves at home like mice in the baseboard, cats behind the curtains, owls in the eaves. Everything will burn: my furniture, my carpets, my paintings, my wardrobe which won't ward off anything at all, my books, my archives, my precious manuscripts, and on top of it all I don't even *like* soup, it's disgusting, I have to force myself to choke it down every time!

A similar escalation marks the conclusion of "Peter and the Wolf," as the associations between instrumental themes and the characters from Prokofiev's orchestral fairy tale go horribly wrong when applied to the works of other composers.

Chevillard is also an extraordinary stylist. His writing

evinces an effortless command of diction and syntax, rhythm and rhyme. There is plasticity to his French, a quality Lydie Salvayre emphasizes when she marvels at how his sentences "roll, accelerate, spin around, walk backward, to end up falling exactly and with a haunting precision just where they should fall—fall, incidentally, is not the word, swoop down would be more accurate."[3] This notion of precision is key: Chevillard is no mere Paganini of the pen, setting off verbal fireworks for the admiration of his public. His playful agility—including the many cases in which his target is the nuance and absurdity of language itself—is consistently matched to its subject matter, infusing French prose with a vitality absent from the kind inhabited by ready-made thought and expression.

Daniel Levin Becker's deft and dexterous rendering of these verbal acrobatics reproduces in English the "untranslatable" wonders of the original. One readily understands why Chevillard writes so admiringly of translators, those advanced technicians of language! It is no easy feat to generate anything like the laughter his original texts provoke in French, relying as they do on the author's ability to fully inhabit and exploit its potential applications (the word *potential* seems especially relevant, given Levin Becker's membership in the Oulipo).

To illustrate my point, let me quote the translator rising to the challenge of a Chevillard line that appeared in one the columns written for *Le Monde* during the lockdown of spring 2020:

> The original is "Tu parles, Charles! Va te faire lanlaire, Baudelaire!" The first half is a common albeit arcane saying, something like "fat chance!"; the second half,

minus the Baudelaire part, is this 19th-century expression of unclear (at least to me) origin that translates roughly to "get lost." So in context, where Chevillard is talking about how naïve he was to think he could resist the influence of the coronavirus on his writing, this isn't actually that complex an idea, just a sort of "Yeah, how's that working out for you?" addressed to himself. But of course, as we've discussed, Chevy's never seen a figure of speech he couldn't sabotage, so he uses Charles Baudelaire to bind the two halves together. At first I wondered if I could get away with replacing Baudelaire with someone else—*Fat chance, Jack! Hit the road, Kerouac!*—but ultimately wasn't confident enough to go out on that limb by myself, so here we are. Rejected alternatives: *like we care, don't you dare, life ain't fair, cut your hair, don't be square.*[4]

Levin Becker's inspired solution—"Good luck, Chuck! Grow a pair, Baudelaire!"[5]—hints at the considerable pleasures in store for the reader of this book.

Not just the quality of writing sets Chevillard apart from so many of his peers but also the refreshingly slant vision behind it. "A style of one's own," notes the novelist and translator Anne Weber,

is as unmistakable as a fingerprint; the poet, his person, the whole of his thought and emotions are suspended in it. I remember when, having just become acquainted with Éric Chevillard and his literature, I encountered the idea in one of his early books that a cock had laid a church there. I looked at the weathercock sitting high up on the church steeple and was startled and touched: was the thought not obvious? Except that it had occurred neither to me nor to

anyone else. About twenty years later I walked with Éric
Chevillard through Stuttgart's pedestrian precinct and past
the bust of Schubert. "Amazing that that man could have
been such a good pianist," Éric said. I looked first at him
and then at Schubert, who was wedged shoulders down in
his stone pedestal.

"It is as if this writer," she concludes, "had a sixth sense allowing him to create analogies where others, mired in their
naïve perceptual habits, see only unconnected objects."[6]

Indeed, quotidian objects are incessantly apprehended
anew in this volume, beginning with household furniture,
be it the chair ("could it be the only truly stationary quadruped?"), the door ("either the door provides passage at a point
in space where there was formerly nothing to impede free
circulation . . . or it forbids access to this or that place by
closing it off"), or the staircase ("what even *is* this useless
piece of furniture cluttering up the house with all its open
overturned drawers?"). Our familiarity with the phenomena
of the natural world is just as quickened by an encounter
with Chevillard's perspective, even those as elemental as sky
("nothing good comes from the sky: not hail, that little buckshot of iceberg . . . nor bombs, nor guano, nor the wrath of
God") and stone ("the stone has it in for us as early as childhood, when it goes after our knees"). Perspectives are re-
versed, considered askew, turned inside out.

Chevillard is a profoundly visual writer and thinker. For
years now he has collaborated with contemporary artists,
notably Philippe Favier, whose images have accompanied
his texts in a variety of settings—including some of the Fata
Morgana books from which the contents of this volume have
been drawn. Chevillard has devoted a monograph to the art

brut painter Gaston Chaissac, whose epigraph adorns his 1994 novel *Prehistoric Times; L'autofictif* contains canny observations of individual artworks from just about every historical period. Several of these shorts are set in museums; in "An Overwhelming Success," he even transforms his own imagination into one. (Incidentally, Chevillard is the best possible companion on a museum visit: I recall my astonishment at the sharpness of his observations during trips to the Frick Collection in New York and the Yale University Art Gallery, his eye alighting on remarkable or odd details hiding in plain sight, with the effortlessness of someone able to instantly spot a four-leaf clover in a field.)

And regardless of what I've referred to as a "diminutive" attitude characteristic of his prose, Chevillard's topics and themes have real urgency. Mischief aside, he has produced a body of writing about animals and ecology that is second to none. The most moving work in this volume is unquestionably "Parliamentary Report," a discourse by one of the seven remaining members of the animal kingdom and an update of Kafka's "Report to an Academy" for the Age of Anthropocene:

> The world without us, Your Excellency, ladies, gentlemen: just try to imagine it. Without the eagle or the horse, without the thirty-three feet of the python snake. No doubt you thought our point of view counted for nothing. But who weighed the fruits in the trees, whose sense organs include radar and sonar and compass, who can smell the coming hurricane, who cries out first when the earth splits open? And who has explored the depths of the ocean, who has tasted the leaves of the jujube? I don't believe I've ever seen you sleep under the grass except when dead, correct

me if I'm wrong. How little you know of this world! You've never danced with an alga. You can't begin to imagine the adventure of life inside a flower. When night falls, you see nothing of this terraqueous globe but its lunatic satellite, while in the same dark we see so many new iridescences, a whole prism of shimmering secondary colors.

Invited to spend a night at a museum of his choice and make it the basis of a long essay, Chevillard stationed himself in the wing of Paris's Gallery of Evolution—a collection of taxidermied animals connected to the National Museum of Natural History—devoted to extinct and endangered species.[7] Elsewhere his novels have imagined disasters ranging from the death of a tortoise to the disappearance of the last orangutan. One of his pandemic columns for *Le Monde* addressed the "Chernobylian Eden" of habitats revived thanks to the temporary retreat of humans during lockdown.[8] During those difficult months, Chevillard's essays and blog were a refuge to me. Their humor, directed at the hardships and fears experienced by so many, felt like armor for the spirit. As in the very best Jewish jokes, his writing, no matter its size and scope, provides momentary respite from the darkness, without diverting from or denying its causes. It delivers its punchlines with something between a grimace and a smile, all the while looking the worst in the eye.

Notes

1. Franz Kafka, "For the Consideration of Amateur Jockeys," in *Metamorphosis and Other Stories*, trans. Michael Hofmann (London: Penguin, 2007).

2. Frédéric Beigbeder, "Halte au chou-fleur!" *Le Figaro,* Novem-

ber 27, 2012; Éric Chevillard, blog post, in *L'autofictif ultraconfidentiel: Journal, 2007–2017* (Talence: L'arbre vengeur, 2018), 684, both quotes translated by Daniel Medin.

3. Lydie Salvayre, "Chevillard; or, The Art of Birlibirloque," trans. Brian Evenson, *Music & Literature* 8 (2017), 121.

4. Michelle Kuo, Jeremy Davies, and Daniel Levin Becker, "Exploding Clichés: On Éric Chevillard's Versatile Prose," *Los Angeles Review of Books,* December 22, 2020.

5. "Éric Chevillard's 'Sine Die': A Coronavirus Story," trans. Daniel Levin Becker, *Music & Literature,* May 28, 2020.

6. Anne Weber, "Final Bouquet," trans. Shaun Whiteside, *Music & Literature* 8 (2017), 140–141.

7. *L'arche Titanic* (Stock, 2021), published in the *Ma nuit au musée* series directed by Alina Gurdiel.

8. "Éric Chevillard's 'Sine Die': Nature Takes Its Course," trans. Daniel Levin Becker, *Music & Literature,* May 7, 2020.

Museum Visits

The Guide

So, right here is where Henri IV ran a hand through his beard, here's where a raindrop landed on Dante's forehead, this is where Buster Keaton bit into a pancake, here Rubens scratched his ear—let's keep moving, please, ladies and gentlemen—here is where the marquise de Sévigné coughed, here Arthur Rimbaud muddied his pants, here Christopher Columbus dropped his hat—stay together, please—here Wolfgang Amadeus Mozart became aware of the fact that magpies always travel in pairs, here Eugène Ionesco broke a shoelace, here Vincent van Gogh combed his hair with his fingers, here Charles Lindbergh grabbed his wife by the waist, here Marcel Proust—*shh!*—used a corner of his handkerchief to remove a bit of dust that was in his eye, here Rivarol stifled a swear word—come to the front, children, you'll see better—here Laozi sniffled, here too, this is where Samuel Beckett turned around, this is where Leonardo da Vinci greeted a man he knew, here Virginia Woolf burst out laughing, here Honoré de Balzac nodded off for a moment, here— watch your step—Johannes Vermeer tripped, here Copernicus hummed, this is where Catherine de' Medici fluttered her eyelashes, this is where Epicurus scratched himself on a bramble, this is where Désiré Nisard sank into obscurity— no farther, please, stay at the edge—here Immanuel Kant took a right, here Napoleon Bonaparte sat down to catch his breath, here François Villon chewed on his thumbnail, here is where Johann Sebastian Bach caught sight of a toad, here Isaac Newton passed by without stopping, here Pablo Picasso ogled the buttocks of a girl who was manifestly too young, this is where George Sand relit her cigar—please put out your cigarettes, this is a no-smoking area now—this is where a very irritated Greta Garbo tossed her hair back, this is where James Joyce wiped the lenses of his eyeglasses, this is where Voltaire crushed a mosquito, here Alexander Graham Bell lost a button and Geronimo picked up a feather, here Aristide Bruant sneezed noisily—mind the drafts—here William Shakespeare stepped on a snail, here Abraham Lincoln touched his forehead, this is where Fragonard put his shoes back on, here André Gide bought a cone of chestnuts, here Hans Christian Andersen wiped away a tear, here Henri Michaux took a photo of a couple of American tourists with their camera—yes, you may, but no flash, please—here Édouard Manet kicked a pebble with his boot, here Raymond Roussel adjusted the knot of his tie, this is where Diane de Poitiers sighed, here Gustave Flaubert cleared his throat, here Ludwig Wittgenstein asked what time it was, which reminds me, please press in closer, ladies and gentlemen, quickly, if you don't mind, this is just the beginning of the visit, we still have a great many places to see . . .

Autofiction

I began ejaculating when I was seven.

It came to me one morning, just like that. I started ejaculating feverishly all over my schoolbooks.

My parents disapproved. You're not old enough to ejaculate. You'll put an eye out.

So what. I continued ejaculating in secret.

I ejaculated, I ejaculated, I ejaculated, without fatigue, without boredom, without deviation, come hell or high water.

I held in my hand a magic wand. I ejaculated certain that I was creating marvelous things.

It was in my blood, to be sure. At the first free moment, did I play with marbles or chase girls? No. I did not watch television. I didn't help my father in the garden. What did I do? I ejaculated.

I used all of my leisure time for ejaculating.

I ejaculated. It was uncontainable.

At sixteen my ejaculations were strongly influenced by Rimbaud, but they weren't very good, now that I think about it.

To be honest, what I ejaculated back then was worthless. Inconsistent. Peanuts. Flan. Eggnog.

But already I took pleasure in it, incredible as that may seem. Ejaculating was my greatest joy.

I devoted my vacations to it. At the age when others went out dancing at night, I was ejaculating.

I got up in the middle of the night to ejaculate.

I ejaculated whatever passed through my head. It didn't go very far.

I started to ejaculate for real around twenty. It became more personal, more substantial. I ejaculated as others might urinate or blow their noses.

I ejaculated my sufferings, my burdens, my solitude.

For I had cut myself off from the world somewhat, ejaculating alone in my room.

It was around this time that I began to want to publicly share what I was ejaculating.

At first, nobody wanted it. Your ejaculations will never interest anyone. It sounds laughable today, of course, and is no doubt difficult to believe, but at first I was often told such things.

You don't have anything good to ejaculate!

You're just not cut out for ejaculating!

Stop ejaculating—now there's a piece of advice I heard more than a few times.

And in fact I almost gave it up. I wanted to try something else. I wanted to vomit, or lay eggs.

But nothing else would do. I had to ejaculate.

It's funny now to think that those people who tried to discourage me are the same ones who today pay me handsomely to ejaculate for them.

Because people literally fight over my ejaculations.

I ejaculate for all the major presses.

I ejaculate in all the major papers.

At this point, I ejaculate wherever I want.

Eminent professors invite their students to study closely what I ejaculate.

And so I have a great demand to fill, and it can be difficult to deliver. Yes, there are times when I drink in order to ejaculate.

And it impacts my home life. My wife feels neglected. Always ejaculating, she says to me sadly.

Won't you stop ejaculating for a moment and hold me in your arms? she sometimes asks me in a quiet little voice.

As if I had nothing else to do. She must understand, though, that in my life ejaculating will always come first.

What can I do? I was born to ejaculate.

It's my livelihood. I have to ejaculate.

I ejaculate mostly at night, but sometimes I also ejaculate straight from morning to evening.

Ejaculate each day, that's my motto.

If for some reason I go for more than twenty-four hours without ejaculating, it pains me. It's awful.

So it doesn't matter where, but I must ejaculate.

I ejaculate on restaurant placemats. I ejaculate on the backs of subway tickets.

Sometimes I even ejaculate on myself.

Everything works, any surface: I can ejaculate on a coaster, in the margins of a newspaper, on a facial tissue.

I prefer to ejaculate by hand rather than directly on the computer.

Yes, I believe ejaculation is a sort of therapy for me, or certainly in any case a sort of catharsis.

All that is repressed comes out when I ejaculate, all the incipient concupiscence.

Ejaculating saved my life, I'm not afraid to say it.

If I hadn't ejaculated I wouldn't be here today.

More than once I have wanted to die, to kill myself—yes—and instead I ejaculated.

And when you ejaculate in a moment like that it is so

good, so powerful, that it practically vibrates from all the emotion held in for too long.

My most recent ejaculation, for instance, I ejaculated in a sort of trance—there's no other word for it. It came all by itself.

I barely had anything to ejaculate, and then it began to gush forth, and there it was.

The whole first part I ejaculated all at once in Ibiza.

I ejaculated the next part in New York.

And I ejaculated the ending at home in Paris, door closed, phone off the hook. I need calm to ejaculate.

It's a burden too, ejaculation. It must be said. Those who are tempted to do it should know that it's not always easy, that it can take a great deal of effort. Sometimes I have to force myself to ejaculate.

So I go ejaculate in a café, or at a library, where there are people around and it's less of a chore than ejaculating in the solitude of the office.

I deny nothing when I ejaculate.

It's been said that my ejaculations convey something universal. It's not hard to see why.

Many people recognize themselves in my ejaculations. It's like a mirror for them. I receive an enormous quantity of mail to this effect.

I am invited with increasing frequency to schools to talk about my ejaculations.

Why do you ejaculate? That's the question I hear most often from the mouths of children.

And I tell them I can't do anything else. For me it is almost a physical, organic need to ejaculate.

Frankly, I'm surprised that anyone can live without ejaculating.

But at the same time, if you ask me, too many people to-day ejaculate. The moment someone becomes slightly famous for this or that reason, they are asked without fail to ejaculate something. I abhor the spread of this practice: in such a profusion of treacle, just try extracting the wheat from the chaff without getting stuck to the floor.

I put my soul and my guts alike into everything I ejaculate: reconciled, unified, almost indistinguishable.

I ejaculate only the truth.

I am suspicious of people who need so many methods and complications to ejaculate.

I'm sorry, but to me that's not ejaculating.

I ejaculate as I breathe.

I ejaculate as I speak.

I ejaculate without worrying about the beauty or the originality of the thing.

I ejaculate because I exist, because I want people to know.

My entire life is in what I ejaculate.

Everything I experience I ejaculate straightaway.

The main challenge is to forget the way we were taught to ejaculate and recapture the innocent joy of that first stroke.

Hear the music of my sentence: *floop.*

The Chair

Yes, but have we ever really asked ourselves what the chair is like in its living state—that is, before the intervention of the upholsterer—have we ever tried to approach the chair in its natural environment, before it's been stuffed and stiffened by rigor mortis and varnish? No? Well maybe that's because we wouldn't dare to sit on it, as we so cavalierly do after it's been rendered harmless! If it were to lash out suddenly, or rear up, or go leaping from rock to rock, branch to branch, bounding across chasms, all of a sudden he'd have much less to boast about, wouldn't he, this seated person.

We know nothing of the chair except when it's grounded, immobilized, taxidermied. Could it be the only truly stationary quadruped? And I don't mean mass migrations, like wildebeest, no no—you never see even a single chair venture so much as a step out of place. Something doesn't add up. The panther can lie in wait too, holding the same position for several minutes as though it's been petrified, but eventually it still pounces. At prey, most often. So what is the chair's prey? What is this prey that it's been stalking for so long, that it will attack instantly on sight? Do you think perhaps it could be *man?*

And yet we voluntarily fling ourselves, several times a

day, into the chair's trap! Sometimes we even sigh in relief as we sink in. And no, the chair doesn't take advantage. It doesn't snap shut around us. Doesn't chop or chew us up. Which must mean it's good and dead, stuffed and mounted like a trophy buck or a bird on a branch. We all but glue an acorn or a hazelnut at its feet. And if we don't, mind you, it's not out of respect for its soul, gone off to be at one with the Great Altogether in the heart of the Great Nothing. None of that Apache claptrap in our house. It's just because we have no idea what it eats.

Acorns, hazelnuts, or perhaps rabbits, slugs, mushrooms, ants? We know nothing about its diet, its reproductive habits, its customs. Is it even diurnal? Haven't we all bumped into one in the dark? Think about it. As for its habitat, we've decided it should share ours, like the cockroach and the cockapoo before it—which just isn't right. It's obviously unhappy here. Why else would it hide under the table the way it does, whenever it can? The truth is we keep it here against its will. The trappers and poachers who make their living trafficking the chair remain tight-lipped about its provenance. Of course they do. All we can say for sure is that it's not found in the desert or on the pack ice—we'd see it otherwise.

In fact, many clues suggest that its biotope is sylvan. The chair is originally from the woods. It's a relative of the tree, even if it's managed to distance itself—more than the swing has, at any rate, although the swing is endowed with the gift of motion, unlike the chair, which, again, doesn't move unless you tackle it. Maybe it trotted here all the way from the forest. Maybe it's winded from the effort, incapable of the slightest movement. Still, it should have caught its breath by now. And this whole time we've known it, it does nothing but rest all day long. On the other hand, it does consistently stand up straight, while for instance the divan droops and the sofa slouches.

Is it really dead, then—or is it just patient, extraordinarily patient? Doesn't it seem to be waiting for something, for something to happen? Maybe its back is the first rung of a ladder, an escape plan at the ready. Upholstered, even re-upholstered, it still poses a threat when you look carefully. There you are in front of it, with that bearing instilled in you by your education, that pride rightly bestowed on you by your labors, that erect stature you acquired in stadiums and weight rooms.

And then you make the mistake of turning your back on it, and that's when, in the space of a second, it breaks you into thirds.

The Museum Visit

Modern man is more predictable than the flowering of the daffodil in the first days of spring. Ask twenty people randomly selected at a museum what they're doing there, and the odds are excellent that all of them, without exception, will tell you they've come to see the works on display and admire the collections. Appalling! Pure conformism aggravated by herd mentality. You'll forgive me if I exclude myself from this category. I am a different species of man. Scarcely, for my part, do I even glance at the paintings hanging on gallery walls. And yet as soon as I arrive in an unfamiliar city I inquire about its museums and then rush to visit them, burning with curiosity, cheeks flushed, in the grips of the most fervent emotion.

For me, the museum visit is a ceaselessly renewed pleasure, perhaps the surest of my enjoyments. The others eventually betray me or corrupt themselves, but this one has never steered me wrong. Let me repeat, though, that it is in no way a love of art that draws me to these places. Art has no justification, in my eyes, besides these museums dedicated to it, which are to the pompous genius of humankind as the pink nacreous shell is to the formless mollusk known as the conch.

I take my place at the end of the endless queue and I wait

as long as I must. Once inside the museum, I keep my head doggedly down. My behavior may be surprising, but since it's neither criminal nor disruptive, strictly speaking, I'm left in peace, plunged into my reflective ecstasies, eyes trained on the ground. I have come for the floors.

I enter the first room and all at once it's as though I've set sail on a galleon or a caravel, those magnificent vessels manned by the conquistadors of the golden age. I cast off my moorings to the sound of swinging masts, pulleys, and chafed wood. Yes, the seascapes on the walls provide a suitable decorative accompaniment for the occasion, albeit a redundant and frankly useless one: the creaking of the floorboards is enough to render perfectly the illusion of the high seas, whereas it's immediately clear that, troubled though it may be by a vigorous brush, the painting isn't *really* water and its wave will remain suspended in the air like a coat on a peg.

Ah, such music beneath my feet! They're bards, these boards. And just as no two lutes make an identical sound at the bard's fingertips, the enthusiast can make every floor groan differently by bearing down on its boards gently or more assertively. You have to know how to play! It's not just porcelain boutiques where the elephant is a liability. How often I am tormented by the ghastly groans that certain oafs pry from these venerable floors on which kings and princesses once danced. You'd think they were stepping on a sow's tail or flattening a mouse with their every step! Such china shops as these should be off-limits to their ungainly hooves.

Some floors crackle like leaves, twigs, and acorns strewn over an autumn undergrowth—we wouldn't be surprised to see a stag scamper off into the receding perspective of the exposition rooms. Others rustle like freshly fallen snow, and, should our imagination allow itself to be bewitched, we can enjoy the sensation of walking knee-deep into the powder. In such moments I may cast an eye over the framed landscapes all around, and if they happen to be winter scenes, frozen lakes or snow-capped mountains, I salute the painter with a discreet bow: he has understood. His work harmoniously inscribes itself in the world. All here is right and clear. These are precious instants, and so rare—for most often, I regret to say, the painting I find offends my eye: another descent from the cross, another burial, some Napoleonic battle scene utterly out of place in this context. The discrepancy shocks my senses like the shriek of chalk on a blackboard. My every nerve revolts. My eye rolls back in its socket, and once again I take the bitter measure of my solitude. The enigma of the world is unbroken, my whole sensory experience brutally invalidated by mute, obtuse reality.

Elsewhere, though, still other floors moan as if to say that the miracle of love can indeed occur, on occasion, beyond the passionate embrace of bodies and the physical exertion that leaves us exhausted and panting in a jumble of bedsheets. Our clothes are not lamentably wrinkled and strewn across these floors; we're even encouraged to keep our shoes on—our shoes being better than our delicate and incurably perverted fingers at coaxing those shrill cries of sensual pleasure that will not, at last, be interrupted by the melancholy of climax, but on the contrary send us crescendoing from room to room until we reach the supreme ecstasy, the absolute harmony of mind and senses finally reconciled.

Hegel's Cap

for Anne Weber

Hegel's cap, preserved in the philosopher's childhood home in Stuttgart, inside a windowed shrine, like a relic, like his brain itself, is, more precisely, a sort of toque, a toque of black velvet that appears in good condition, barely greening after nearly two centuries, though of course we'd have to be able to turn it over to examine the other side, the inside, eroded or singed, perhaps, by the overheated cogitation of the author of *Phenomenology of Spirit,* pot-roasted by the incessant ebullition of his intellect, or at least greasy from his hair; a toque that has, at its center, or its summit, like a pom-pom—though given the grave questions of morality and law debated beneath it, said pom-pom would have been entirely inappropriate—a second patch, round in shape, and brighter, barely yellowing for its part after almost two centuries, made from the same very fine, very soft velvet, and stitched with golden thread.

It's something to be seen.

It's something to be seen, this cap. It is already, in itself, by its own virtues, without Hegel beneath or inside it, quite impressive. Let's face it, we no longer wear hats like this, nor do philosophers still make use of them. Now, neither do philosophers still formulate concepts as powerful and compelling as those that took shape in Hegel's brain, not since they gave up—for reasons that remain obscure, come to think of it—wearing this kind of cap while they ruminated. I'm not claiming these things are related. I'm merely, dispassionately, positing a coincidence. Besides, what would it cost for one of our trendy modern philosophers to give it a try, to don a cap of the same model, a toque-like number in black velvet and topped with a brighter patch—why not this cap, Hegel's cap, with the permission of the conservator or, boldly, without it, a first audacity that would be well worth appreciating—and then wait, beneath or inside it, for ideas to come, and then weigh up their pertinence, evaluate their originality? Will no one, none of our trendy modern philosophers, venture to try at least this?

I don't regret having seen it.

I don't regret having seen this cap. It's heavy and wide, soft and sagging, but all the same this is the cap that covered the egg that was Hegel's head, that brooded it for as long as the ideas took to germinate and then hatch, until all eight hundred pages of the *Phenomenology of Spirit* were written in their entirety. It's a cloche cap, a cap that covered Hegel's head in full and almost certainly flattened his hair— how comical it must have been when he took it off in the evenings—but also almost certainly prevented his thoughts from roaming or rambling outside the orbit of his skull, thereby facilitating, when necessary, his faculties of concentration. Nothing got out of there except through Hegel's mouth or hand.

You have to have seen it.

You have to have seen it, then, this cap, in Stuttgart, in its reliquary. It's a moving testament, a concrete trace of Hegel's thought, the substrate or precipitate of his philosophy. Not to mention proof that he was, moreover, a man like us, sensitive to nips and chills, concerned with his comfort and with his elegance too, even if we've come quite a long way on the latter point since the early nineteenth century and it would no longer occur to any of us to wear such a hat for the sake of elegance. But then of course there are many ideas that no longer occur to any of us, not since we stopped wearing caps like this for fear of ridicule.

Then I went back.

I went back one year later, to Hegel's childhood home, in Stuttgart, to see, once more, in particular, his black velvet cap with the patch stitched in golden thread, and I was wrong to. I've made a few mistakes in my life, and this was one of them. You have to have seen it, this cap, I don't take that back—but once is enough. And even the first time you don't need to linger in front of the windowed shrine. You can just walk by. And nothing says you can't quicken your step, either. You can just take a quick look at Hegel's greenish velvet cap with a yellowing patch on top. A distracted glance, cast without stopping, is sufficient to appreciate the lesson, and to meditate on it, in the same stride that carries you briskly away from the reliquary. And the mistake not to make—the mistake that I nonetheless made—is to go back. To be completely honest, the second visit is redundant. Even the first time, now that I think about it, the second second already felt long. Boredom was creeping in. A visit to Hegel's cap is an experience like so many others: it should remain singular.

You can go once to kill some time if you have absolutely nothing better to do in Stuttgart.

Stones

I'm sorry, but are we going to have to put up with this much longer, the permanent, pervasive presence of stones? Are we so tender and brittle that we must forever and everywhere stumble and scrape ourselves on stones, fall flat and founder over them, let them damage our delicate skin and the even more sensitive suede that covers it? Because that's what we really are, for stones: fountains of blood waiting to spurt forth, skeletons made of matchsticks. Yet another one of those unreported scandals to which we're supposed to resign ourselves. Well I say no! No, I do not resign myself to this! The stone has it in for us as early as childhood, when it goes after our knees. We are wrong to speak of its stillness. The stone rolls, the stone flies; like the fist, it avails itself of, arms itself with, the hand that launches it.

When it comes to rest, it's only to petrify this impenetrable, infertile, inhospitable world in its image. Our drilling implements pierce its crust and unearth still more stone. We're weighed down by stones our whole lives, like a corpse after a rape and thirty-six stab wounds. No wonder we're so earthbound. Each stone is ultimately a gravestone, right down to the lid that tumbled, clamorous as a landslide, over the tomb of that nice man who was smashed to pieces by incessant stoning and refused to fight back.

What are they really, stones, if not rubble carelessly left behind by the Creator of Heaven and Earth? He couldn't even be bothered to clean up his construction site, so now it's our responsibility, alongside so many other miseries. Garbage, just garbage: detritus, remains, ruins preordained from the outset, the squalid precipitate of pitchy sedimentations. And a few random successes, a few precious crystalline concretions—which are also, for that matter, responsible for their fair share of severed fingers—won't make us forget the trenchant ridges, the acute angles, the surly roughness of the rocks scattered everywhere. Even the ocean uses all its patience and all its furor to turn stones into pebbles—still far from fruity under our rodent teeth—to the exclusion of so many nobler, more useful tasks we could have assigned it.

And so? What to do, unthinkable as it is to let this situation stand forever? I see only one solution: clear it all away! Haul off the stones! We'll stack them up on the moon—it's not like the moon will be any deader for it. A tough row to hoe, I don't deny it. But also what a dent we'll be making in the future, what a world of possibilities suddenly opened up! A world without stones, where we will roam freely, unshod, over carpets of grass and moss, moved to the very soles of our feet by the newfound gentleness of things.

History of the
Peloponnesian War

It costs me dearly to confess it—shame! shame on me and my laziness and my narrow mind!—but I must come clean: *History of the Peloponnesian War* bores me so profoundly that without fail it falls from my hands, and does so with a great crashing din, the work—unfinished, thankfully—numbering eight volumes. I gather them up. I put them back in order. I make another attempt that will end in another fiasco. Each time I wind up dismally astray, tripped up or bogged down, and after a few pages of tedious and absent effort I give up. When the name Thucydides is uttered in my presence, I turn red from embarrassment, wishing the ground would open up and swallow me. I can almost hear the snickering crowd, mocking and scornful. And yet honesty compels me to admit it: *History of the Peloponnesian War* will soon be the only volume in our libraries to escape my vast and punctilious erudition. For you would be wrong to think my lack of interest spans the entire corpus of ancient Greek historiography. By no means! Each day I spend a few hours absorbed in Xenophon's *Anabasis,* during which time nothing else can distract me. My copy of Eratosthenes of Cyrene's *Chronographies* is more worn out than the old miller's old donkey, and I've annotated my Herodotus so much that the main text could pass for a succinct, sometimes even perfunctory gloss of my marginal commentary. Even Eusebius's *Ecclesiastical History* sends me into quivering fits of laughter, which my lady friends observe with a certain anxiety as they snap their suitcases shut. As a rule, when invited to dinner, I bring my hosts the inexhaustible *Hellenica* of Theopompus instead of the perennial ephemeral bouquet of flowers or bottle of wine that won't last the evening. And should you see me crying alone in the street, it's not because disease is clawing its way through my entrails like a feral mole, nor because the bitterness of our condition has mingled once again in my alembics with the elixir of life or love potion (from which I expected more, I admit, than these devastating explosions, this mephitic smoke, this powdery ash over everything): no, I'm crying because we've lost the *Life of Philopoemen* by Polybius, and nothing can ever bring it back. And still—I'll say it again—no suffering in this world afflicts me more than not being able to read more than three pages of the *History of the Peloponnesian War:* not even the impossible gesticulations of the limbless torso-man are as lamentable as my flailing breaststroke through Thucydides' masterpiece, that pitiless mirror of my stupidity, my ignorance, my negligence, that dark tomb of my hopes and ambitions. For it is there, in truth, in Athens or Sparta, in 404 BCE, that death awaits me. Ah! May it take me at last and deliver me from my shame!

The Certificate

I fear it may be too late, yet I can't bring myself to sit idly by. Michel Nolleau, poor little wretch! How can I allow such injustice to persist when it's within my power to set the record straight? For I have, by the sheerest chance, come into possession of a document that exonerates him and could therefore change his life, perhaps even his eternal life, yes, his lowly lot among the deceased, if he's dead: a document he appears to have mislaid some forty-five years ago, the loss of which no doubt brought heavy consequences down upon him, upon his frail little chicken-body, upon his plucked and quivering soul.

I dare not imagine these consequences. In spite of myself, however, the depiction of hell by the painters of the Renaissance comes to mind.

Woebegone little Nolleau! And even if he's not dead yet—the document is dated 1959, and he must have been about ten at the time, which would make him somewhere around sixty-five years old at the moment I'm writing these words, though of course the moment I'm writing these words has already passed—what turn must his life have taken, what turn of the screw, what irremediably ruinous turn? Into what hellish spiral was he plunged, dead or alive, after losing this document?

It must have slipped from his pocket or his missal, float-ing for a few moments over the cold streets as this carefree scamp, his Sunday duties accomplished, returned to his res-idence with clogs clacking. And what a lashing must have awaited him upon his arrival, when his parents asked to see the certificate and he couldn't produce it!

Blows rained down on his back, on his loins, on the nape of his neck. Pitiful little Nolleau pleading his good faith—in vain. In the absence of the document, they didn't be-lieve him. A certificate more precious than an identity card, clearly, the kind of attestation you'd do best to stitch over your heart, never leaving home without it or letting it out of your sight for any reason whatsoever. When you're bathing? Nestle it in your armpit. When you're fucking? No fucking.

So, this Sunday, March 15, 1959, that thousandfold-accursed day, Michel Nolleau lost—for me to discover again today in an attic, between the pages of a novel whose content is no less threadbare than its paper and binding—this certificate which every honest man carries on his person at all times—it may be, in fact, that the narrow cleft of our buttocks, which can carry neither books nor bundles, has devolved to this sole purpose: to hold tightly between its two gluteal mounds, making it pos-sible for us to produce and display it at any moment should the need arise, this unique document which Michel Nolleau found himself so dramatically lacking when it was required of him: the Certificate of Mass Attendance.

It is a little yellowish slip of paper with that title, which was to be renewed each quarter and which bears, printed in a grid, the dates of all the season's Sundays and, next to each one, a blank space to accommodate the signature of the parish priest at the end of mass—it would have been too easy to register one's attendance before the service started, then scamper off to roust birds from the hedges and gobble down their little white- or blue-flecked eggs. We know their kind, those naughty scamps! Having noted the presence of the faithful young parishioner—dogs too are faithful, as we know, especially when they're also chained to an iron ring— the priest would append his initials to the loyalty card. Then he would demand oral gratification amid the incense-and-cold-wax odor of the sacristy.

Was little Nolleau subjected to this as well? I can't affirm it with certainty at this stage in my investigation, but I'm not ruling out any hypotheses. All we know for sure is he lost his Certificate of Mass Attendance, God damn it all! And that it was picked up by a passerby, who, instead of returning it to its owner in proper Christian fashion, used it as a bookmark for her own profane readings. From then on, Michel was unable to prove his diligent attendance, first to his parents—it would take more to convince them than a splotch of dried sperm on his collar, that could be from anyone— who very likely gave him a sound thrashing—not only had he missed mass, but where had he been, the little urchin, in what reprehensible and sinful acts was he indulging under the cover of that pious alibi?—and second, if he's dead, to the saints at the gates of heaven, who surely insist on seeing that admit-one invitation, since they can't monitor everybody or remember everything, and thus sent him pitilessly away.

Weep for little Nolleau! For he was, in truth, a very assiduous subject of the good Lord, His most devoted servant. And I am now in a position to prove it, to provide the case-closing evidence that chanced to fall into my hands, this Certificate of Mass Attendance, God damn it all, confirming, as evidenced by the signature of the Beauvoir parish priest, that little Michel Nolleau did not miss a single service in 1959, at least not until that fateful March 15.

Not only that: on January 25 and February 22 of that year, Michel Nolleau also, without being obligated—*for fun,* as we would say today—even attended Vespers! What little boy in the present day could boast such devotion? And poor little Nolleau, because he had lost his Certificate of Mass Attendance, was surely scorned by his classmates as a heretic, a heathen, a renegade, an apostate—Infidel dog! they shouted at him in the schoolyard. Later, he never married. The church banned him from its ranks, perhaps even excommunicated him. And to top it all off, if he's dead, he was damned!

O, pity on poor Michel Nolleau! Have pity! Don't tell me judgments can't be appealed in the court of God either! I have the certificate! Here it is! Look at it! We must wrest Nolleau from the depths of hell where he unjustly rots. We must deliver him from the devouring flames, we must cleanse his besmirched honor, we must exonerate him! No doubt he deserves a place among our religion's sacred martyrs, to the right of Our Heavenly Father.

Let us place his little bones in a reliquary shrine, his skull on a cushion of crimson velvet, brothers, let us kneel before the remains of little Nolleau, and pray that his soul find peace and our sins be forgiven.

Pascale Frémondière and Sylvie Masson

Since the beginning of the year, the teacher has mixed up Pascale Frémondière and Sylvie Masson. He gets it wrong each time, without fail. When he addresses one, he names the other. He gives Pascale Frémondière's homework back to Sylvie Masson, and to Pascale Frémondière he gives Sylvie Masson's. Sylvie Masson, come to the blackboard! he orders, looking at Pascale Frémondière. Pascale Frémondière, the floor is yours, he says to Sylvie Masson.

The laws of probability do not apply here. The teacher could get it right one time out of two, by luck. By chance. But never. When he speaks to his colleagues of Sylvie Masson, he has Pascale Frémondière in mind. And when the topic of Pascale Frémondière comes up, it's Sylvie Masson he's thinking of. Or rather he's thinking of both, one merged with the other—he doesn't differentiate. Sylvie Masson, Pascale Frémondière, same thing, harmless young ladies.

Pascale Frémondière and Sylvie Masson are two young ladies with short brown hair. They are not very tall or very flamboyant. But Sylvie Masson and Pascale Frémondière don't look alike. Pascale Frémondière has bright eyes and a straight nose. Whereas Sylvie Masson has dark eyes and a hooked nose. Also, Sylvie Masson wears glasses. Not Pascale

Frémondière, who wants to be an airline pilot. These are distinguishing traits, after all.

The teacher could pay attention. He could make an effort. There is a certain scorn evinced by this perpetual confusion, when you think about it. The teacher denies Sylvie Masson. He denies Pascale Frémondière. The teacher doesn't accept that there is on one hand Pascale Frémondière and on the other Sylvie Masson. He wants there to be only one of them, whom he will call sometimes Sylvie Masson, sometimes Pascale Frémondière. Without thinking, he opts for Pascale Frémondière or for Sylvie Masson. For him it is a matter of no consequence.

Pascale Frémondière or Sylvie Masson, honestly, what's the difference? What distinguishes them, these two beings, besides a pair of glasses? One or the other, who really cares? Sylvie Masson or Pascale Frémondière, interchangeable. The teacher isn't about to devote his scarce leisure time to the comparative study of Pascale Frémondière and Sylvie Masson. He has better things to do! That's not the topic of his thesis. "Extant Differences Between Sylvie Masson and Pascale Frémondière." Excuse him for working to untangle more exciting enigmas.

He has freed a slot in his memory for Pascale Frémondière and Sylvie Masson, which is already plenty. They'll be perfectly fine there together. Sylvie Masson and Pascale Frémondière, so happy to be not entirely ignored. In the neighboring slots—like friends, like brothers—Rimbaud, Mozart, Shakespeare. It would be rich indeed for them to complain! The teacher refuses to weigh down his brain with useless information, trifling nuances. Between Pascale Frémondière and Sylvie Masson, knowing which one is Sylvie Masson and which Pascale Frémondière, what's the point? Talk about a useless piece of knowledge that will never come in handy. You'll never find an opportune moment to trot it out in conversation, much less a lecture.

And yet it would suffice for him to learn to recognize one in order to know immediately who the other is. By deduction. By elimination, if he prefers. Recognizing Sylvie Masson, he would call her Sylvie Masson. Not recognizing her, he would call her Pascale Frémondière. In fact, there are quite few points in common between Sylvie Masson and Pascale Frémondière. Not for nothing does each have a name and a face. Upon closer inspection, *everything* distinguishes them. You wouldn't know where to begin yoking one to the other. But the teacher doesn't care. He doesn't even not care, in fact. It doesn't concern him at all. The least of his worries, intolerable little runt that it is, causes him greater problems.

And then the accident. A car veers off the road. Pascale Frémondière was in it. Farewell, Pascale Frémondière, who is now to be buried. The teacher has made a point of attending. His expression is serious, solemn, pained. How cruel, death, says his forehead. He moves slowly, with care. He kneels before the open tomb. He crosses himself. He has lowered his head. You would swear he was praying. At last he stands. He gathers himself up, a rose in his hand. He really is quite elegant. Then he takes a step forward. In a broad but precise motion, he throws the rose into the grave, onto the coffin of Sylvie Masson.

The Sky

The sky! The sky, my friends! I suppose we're damned to have the sky over our heads at all times, nobody saying anything about it, nobody taking offense. We lift up our eyes, and what do we see? The sky! And not just a corner, not just an angle, no: the sky all the way across, from one end to the other, perhaps even beyond! Yet another fait accompli, a brute fact we're supposed to accept calmly and docilely. But what a bore, this sky that's always there and not nearly as ever-changing as they say! And what can we do but send our grievances up into this bluish, matterless abyss, where they'll just be irretrievably lost?

I say matterless because you couldn't call it consistent, that flabby cloud stupidly sailing along up there, assuming the shape of a daffodil and then a dill pickle and then a cul-de-sac and then a sack of potatoes, before suddenly bursting into a rainfall crackling over our crania—which, unlike ducks' heads, are so often exposed to these inundations due to a manly baldness—a result of the cerebral overheating we require to elaborate our boldest conceptions and bitterest philosophies—and due to our lack of fins, unless you count our ears, which are so far from watertight that we overhear everything ever murmured about us.

Nothing good comes from the sky: not hail, that little

buckshot of iceberg, nor the blunt-force meteor, nor the lightning that roasts us where we stand, like potatoes who have forsaken the protection of the sack, nor bombs, nor guano, nor the wrath of God.

And manna? you're saying.

True, there is manna.

Indeed, there is manna. Why load up a basket of provisions to take on a picnic in the countryside when we can count on manna, the munificent rain of manna that will surely fall upon us, into our wide-open mouths, the very moment we're hungry, after which we'll treat ourselves to a nice little digestive siesta at the foot of an oak tree with our hands crossed over our rounded bellies?

It turns out, owing no doubt to a series of unfortunate happenstances, a scarcely believable run of bad luck, that I have personally never been gratified by a rain of manna.

Never! And this miserliness toward me, you will understand, only sharpens the pique, the hatred the sky awakens in me. And the prospect of having to stay there after I shuffle off this mortal coil only redoubles my bias against death—for I have no desire to wander among pale and puffy clouds into a dizzy dazzle of blinding light.

So what to do? I see only one solution: ceilings! Let us build them everywhere, all the way across. Let us continue the admirable work we've started in our individual dwellings. Let us build ceilings between ceilings and connect these ceilings to one another until we can no longer see this sky so covetous of our souls and thoughts. Let us work together toward a skyless world in which we will go forth, bareheaded, under the robust shelter of our roof beams, moved from the arches of our feet up by the newfound gentleness of things.

The Harpsichord

I learn from the concert program, handed out at the chapel's entrance, that we were born the same year, the harpsichordist and I. But that he discovered a passion for the music of Bach when he was ten. We were born the same year, and here we are at last, reunited in the same space, a chapel—which is a hell of a stroke of luck, since, while I'm sure his professional obligations bring him often to such places, I practically never set foot therein. And yet, incontestably, here we are before one another, he onstage at the altar and me, sitting in the audience, in the back row, waiting—and what does he do?

He starts playing the harpsichord!

We were born the same year, forty years ago at that. Never before this evening had we met. Our bodies had never crossed paths, or if so then only fleetingly, in the ruckus of a pedestrian street or at a train station. Unbeknownst to us. Today is the first time since we've been on this earth that our destinies have so perfectly coincided. Behind us the infinite meanders of our respective trajectories that never once overlapped; now, all of a sudden, the same floor under our feet, the same vault of bare stones over our heads. Our paths, miraculously, have been superimposed. Our two existences, his and mine, have led us to this place, to this moment. And would you believe it, what is he doing?‍

He's playing the harpsichord!

Nineteen sixty-four, nineteen sixty-five, nineteen sixty-six, nineteen sixty-seven, nineteen sixty-eight, nineteen sixty-nine, nineteen seventy, nineteen seventy-one, nineteen seventy-two, nineteen seventy-three, nineteen seventy-four, nineteen seventy-five, nineteen seventy-six, nineteen seventy-seven, nineteen seventy-eight, nineteen seventy-nine, nineteen eighty, nineteen eighty-one, nineteen eighty-two, nineteen eighty-three, nineteen eighty-four, all these years, we have known each of them, he and I, and each of the days that made them up. We lived through them all, unwavering contemporaries. In spite of which, what does he do?

He plays the harpsichord!

As if I weren't here, with him, in this chapel. As if I had not also traversed all those years to arrive here, as if I too hadn't had to make it to the end of each, one by one, day after day, from daybreak to sundown and then the whole night long. He was alive somewhere, just as I too, courageously, lived. For much of this time he was practicing the harpsichord, I assume, which also explains why we didn't meet earlier. I don't recall having any relationship with that instrument whatsoever, neither during my childhood nor afterward. A bit like the hunting horn, if you will, which is at least one thing shared by these two instruments that you never see together—that's right, not even these days, when more and more things are connected. But he, it would seem, has his own idea of harmony.

Imperturbably, he plays the harpsichord.

He plays his piece quite diligently. His body rocks gently, from front to back, then front again. The harpsichord is narrow, made of a light wood. You can almost hear the chime of metal on crystal. Astonishing, this combination sewing machine–dishwasher, I muse to myself, every home should have one. I am angry at the harpsichordist for not understanding. He believes the miracle here is his music and not the fantastic coincidence of our meeting. But then I didn't wait for him to discover Bach, even if I wasn't yet playing him at ten years old (back then all that mattered to me was Virgil, Virgil, Virgil, you know children and their exclusive tastes). Rigid and rocking on his stool, the harpsichordist plays his chords without brooking the slightest distraction. I can think of only two words for my contemporary: *sourpuss* and *churl.*

Isn't he playing the harpsichord?

Nineteen eighty-five, nineteen eighty-six, nineteen eighty-seven, nineteen eighty-eight, nineteen eighty-nine, nineteen ninety, nineteen ninety-one, nineteen ninety-two, nineteen ninety-three, nineteen ninety-four, nineteen ninety-five, nineteen ninety-six, nineteen ninety-seven, nineteen ninety-eight, nineteen ninety-nine, two thousand, two thousand one, two thousand two, two thousand three, two thousand four, only by reading each of these years one by one can you even begin to imagine the duration, all the time we've spent together on this earth, the harpsichordist and I. And yet he seems barely concerned. He's going about his own business, as though there were nothing else going on. And what is he doing? Ah yes.

He's playing the harpsichord.

Forty summers have gone by, forty springs, forty autumns, forty winters, forty July fifteenths, for instance, and forty February fifteenths, forty November twenty-fourths, forty supposed Christmas holidays, and there we were, both of us, the harpsichordist and I, on this earth. Whereas in nineteen fifty-nine neither he nor I was here; even in nineteen sixty-three you could have spent days looking for us—he wasn't there. Nor I, I wasn't there either. We made our appearance simultaneously, suddenly, the same year out of all the innumerable years in all the innumerable centuries: he, the harpsichordist, and I, currently seated before him, this person who apparently doesn't know how to do anything but this.

Play the harpsichord.

For the first time we are breathing the same air; for the first time we are enveloped by the same light, sheltered by the same roof. You might believe we've lived for no reason but to wind up here, today. We no longer need to run, to struggle. We'll no longer leave tracks behind us like hunted foxes. We can lay down our baggage. We have *found* each other. And yet the harpsichordist remains concentrated on his little song. He doesn't appear to realize that we'll never see each other again. Two thousand five, two thousand six, two thousand seven . . . we will resume our ridiculous race, each on his own, most likely for the length of the life we have left to live, he and I, which will perhaps be equal, his and mine, as would be more or less logical. We could have enjoyed this moment of respite.

But he'd rather play the harpsichord.

Whatever happens, we will no longer be here, on this earth, in two thousand seventy-five, neither he nor I—to be conservative, very conservative, for it's not totally certain either that we'll reach the age of one hundred ten, even if we obviously can't exclude the possibility altogether. If we do, perhaps chance will place us in each other's presence again, once or twice. I doubt it. I don't frequent harpsichord concerts. For that matter, I wonder what I'm doing at this one. I won't be caught at one again. If there's one place where we don't have even the slenderest chance of crossing paths in the future, it's definitely harpsichord concerts. And unless he runs into me on a street corner, I hardly see what circumstance will bring us together. We will have known each other for only two hours out of our existence, and this is what it will boil down to.

He will have played the harpsichord.

A truck slows on the street in front of the chapel. An orange beam from its emergency light, diffracted by the small tiles of the stained glass, slides over the walls. For a few minutes, the clamor of the trash collectors, the scrape of garbage cans on the asphalt, the fracas of waste tumbling into the dumpster, these offer a comical counterpoint to the harpsichordist's pretentious chiming, his obstinate hammering—

falsely perky, finally maddening, unbearable. I am secretly delighted. May I swiftly be lost in space, far from him, as before, in utter ignorance of his existence, whether he live or die. We have no business at all with one another, I'm more certain of it with each passing moment. Nothing at all. And nonetheless, never has a mistaken impression been set to such appropriate music.

(Shall I admit that I don't much care for the tart sound of the harpsichord? I admit it.)

Peter and the Wolf

Fine, yes, fine, *Peter and the Wolf* is charming, I don't deny it. It's a suitable introduction to orchestral music for the infantile target audience of this unseemly and tedious manifestation of human genius, this fireworks display of polished brass and varnished wood, this spectacle of severe characters dressed in black, waggling their mallets, their batons, their drumsticks, their bows, as though it weren't enough for humankind to have mastered the shovel, the crankshaft, the saw, the ladle, and the oyster fork. Sergei Prokofiev deemed, with a mélange of mischief, trickery, and accuracy, that it was necessary to bamboozle these little scamps lest they moan and groan and make a ruckus if not opportunely distracted, by a little trifle of a tale, from this dour, starchy symphonic insipidity.

And so, as we know—how could we not?—he had the bright idea of assigning to each character in the story an orchestral instrument and a musical phrase so that the unsuspecting child, ignominiously manipulated and silenced, would stay in his seat without wriggling all over the place. Thus the strings introduce Peter, the joyous and smiling little hero; the light and chirping flute introduces the bird, the melancholic oboe the duck, the clarinet the cat on velvet paws, the severe and somber horns the wolf, the rumbling bassoon the grumbling grandfather, the timpani and the bass drum the hunters. The story is simple: Peter disobeys his grandfather and goes adventuring in the countryside, where he meets a cat, a bird, and a duck who all set about haranguing each other musically. Later, a wolf devours the duck. Peter, perched on a branch, captures the wolf thanks to the bird and a rope, the hunters who had been tracking it arrive too late, and the whole affair turns into a perfectly orchestrated commotion of collective jubilation.

A reader narrates this pleasant story, none of which the audience would understand if all we had to go by was the narrative expressiveness of the music—but anyway it's bright, upbeat, potent. As children, we have three or four occasions to hear this concert, then several more to see its cartoon adaptations. Now not a Christmas, not a birthday goes by without a music-loving (not to say curmudgeonly) aunt gifting us a new recording on compact disc: *Peter and the Wolf,* them again, starring this or that suave-voiced actor as the narrator. All of them must play this role sooner or later, no escaping it: it's the hallmark of a successful career, along with Hamlet and Don Juan.

But there's the rub: clubbed over the head with *Peter and the Wolf*—saturated, lobotomized—the child winds up permanently and irrevocably identifying the instruments with the characters they arbitrarily represent in that story. I myself am a victim of this very syndrome, and now music is forever ruined for me. Because if it obviously works with the tale tailormade for Prokofiev's instrumental piece, it absolutely does not for other pieces in the classical repertoire. Nonetheless, you must understand, to me the rumbling bassoon will always be a grumbling grandfather, the melancholic oboe a duck, the sweet clarinet a cat on velvet paws, the bass drum a hunter, the severe and somber horn a wolf emerging from the woods, and the violin that joyous and smiling rascal Peter.

So just imagine the nightmarish images visited upon me when I hear, for instance, Tchaikovsky's *Symphonie pathétique:* the melancholic duck eats the eyes of the cat on velvet paws, who dies while clawing out joyous and smiling Peter's stomach. Then the grumbling grandfather marries the melancholic duck, while the hunters kill each other and the light and chirping bird carries the severe and somber wolf off to devour him in its aerie! And Mahler's *Song of the Night:* the severe and somber wolf is the finance minister, who passes a law condemning the velvet-footed cat to a life of shelling peas. The light and chirping bird vomits wallpaper glue. Joyous and smiling Peter plucks the melancholic duck alive, and the hunters slaughter the grandfather while he grumbles in his bathtub. Awful as this is, it's nothing compared to what happens in Beethoven's *Pastoral Symphony:* joyous and smiling Peter rapes his grumbling grandfather, the cat on velvet paws has become an alcoholic, the light and chirping bird and the melancholic duck appear only in the form of pâtés three days past their expiration date, and the severe and somber wolf and the hunters divvy up the world like quarters of an orange. And Ravel's *Bolero!* An abomination! The severe and somber wolf passes himself off as the cat on velvet paws, who is pretending to be the light and chirping bird, who is impersonating joyous and smiling Peter, who fancies himself a hunter, who turns out to be the grumbling grandfather of the melancholic duck. And when it's done, it starts all over again. Debussy's *Prelude to the Afternoon of a Faun* is a mortifying ordeal for me. And Berlioz's *Symphonie fantastique* is nothing but a succession of unnatural acts, a sordid and macabre delirium I would prefer not to describe. There might be children listening.

Parliamentary Report

Mister President, ladies, gentlemen, I won't pretend to be daunted to find myself here before you, addressing this assembly. I have experienced far more difficult things, believe me. There are only seven of us left and we let chance determine who would be the emissary of the group. It fell to me. So I made the journey. Don't ask me how. The path is secret and I intend to take it again, in the opposite direction, to rejoin my kind once I've told you what I have to tell you.

Learning your language was not difficult. Aren't we known for our talents of imitation? I can also mimic the sirens of your cargo ships, the whir of your airplane engines, the sharp little click of your hedge clippers. But I haven't come to distract or amuse you. The time for that has come and gone as well. The performance is over. Curtains!

There are only seven of us left, five males and two females. The converse would have been more advantageous, with respect to our chances of survival, I mean, but that too is beyond our control. We have always been peaceable toward you. You had to actually stick your arm deep inside our burrow for us to bite you. Or fall between our teeth fully roasted, when the battlefields were strewn with your bodies and it was left to us to clean up. We didn't come looking to provoke you. We didn't chase you. It's been you, always you, who opened hostilities. You brandished your whips, you launched your harpoons, you shouldered your rifles.

You tracked us everywhere, Your Majesty, ladies, gentlemen. Into the darkest forest where we made our den, you cast the cold light of your ax. You carved a stairway into the water, leading down to the unfathomable abysses where we made our refuge. You hoisted yourself onto the forest canopy and left behind the greasy papers of your picnics. You climbed to the summit of the steep mountain where we built our nest, you slithered into the galleries where we tucked away our larvae. You took from us the hollow trunk and the *Madrepora,* the bush and the river. All we have left is the rainbow.

Don't misunderstand me: I'm not here to ask for your sympathy. We know that you save your tears to season your sorrows and baptize your dead, that you weep only for yourselves and when you do it's a veritable downpour, so much so that we wonder how your feet can stink like they do. And it's not because of our exceptional sense of smell that we know this. Mighty trees also wither at your approach. No, I'm not hoping for your sympathy. Your compassion is a burden to us anyway, as much as your so-called caresses, as when you scratch our head with your fingernail, when you pat us on the rump. It took the recent advent of sex toys for you to ease up on your suffocating embraces. You should know how tired we were of rubbing ourselves on cactuses to rehabilitate our fur soiled with drool and spunk.

I'm not here to sweet talk. I haven't come to beg either. Your claims are staked and I have nothing to leverage against them. So I won't wear myself out sounding my trill, I won't lift a load fifty times my body weight, and I won't make a forty-foot jump or turn the color of this podium or make my scales sparkle.

In any case, that's not what it is about us that makes you so covetous. Our treasures are a trifle to you. If you've poached us, harpooned us, exterminated us, if there are only seven of us left today, two females and five males, ladies, gentlemen, it's been so you could dress yourselves up in our feathers. You want our ivory and our amber. Our horn, when powdered, adds a touch of spice to your dismal sex lives. Had you asked us nicely, we would have been only too happy to stick it in your slits ourselves. At three tons going thirty miles an hour, we would have helped you find new and deeper orifices for your pleasure! I can imagine, of course, that our performances in that realm are dazzling to you, but you must understand: our multiple litters, our fabulous begettings, are not enough to compensate for the way your slaughters have slashed our numbers. You sever our hands to make ashtrays, you tear out our spikes to make your pick-up sticks and our teeth to carve your paunchy idols into, and still you're offended when from time to time we bite you on the buttock.

But I haven't come to threaten you, Great Sachem, Your Honor, Very Holy Father, forgive me, I am not yet wise to all your airs and graces; your presence excites the defense reflexes in my anal gland, ladies and gentlemen, and you too, Most Serene Highness. I am only defending myself, not threatening you. Besides, you don't need our beak or our claws to tear yourselves from head to toe. I must say, in your defense, that you don't go easy on yourselves either. You cough alongside us in the cloud produced by your overheated brains. You've set fire to the sky, the sea ice is crumbling, we're all adrift on an iceberg that soon won't even be large enough to cool your whiskey. Each of Your Lordships belches more smoke than a volcano, and you have the gall to justify your massacres by calling us nuisances and parasites! Who's more contagious, I ask you? We die of *your* flu. Mad human disease drops us from our treetops. Ladies and gentlemen, your hands are implacable shears, sickles, scythes; my friends, the forest shrinks away when you appear. It's afraid of you! The desert follows on your heels as you spread sand behind you to mark the way back to your empty house, your dead garden, your solitude.

I have come before this assembly to roar, to trumpet, to ululate in order to save you. Because we pity you, you must know, because we are well placed to show you the horror of a world without us, this bleak humans-only enclosure whose bars you are forging as we speak. Talk about a zoo that will want for visitors. You'll have to count on the tapeworm, which you'll end up loving. Beggars can't be choosers.

The world without us, Your Excellency, ladies, gentlemen: just try to imagine it. Without the eagle or the horse, without the thirty-three feet of the python snake. No doubt you thought our point of view counted for nothing. But who weighed the fruits in the trees, whose sense organs include radar and sonar and compass, who can smell the coming hurricane, who cries out first when the earth splits open? And who has explored the depths of the ocean, who has tasted the leaves of the jujube? I don't believe I've ever seen you sleep under the grass except when dead, correct me if I'm wrong. How little you know of this world! You've never danced with an alga. You can't begin to imagine the adventure of life inside a flower. When night falls, you see nothing of this terraqueous globe but its lunatic satellite, while in the same dark we see so many new iridescences, a whole prism of shimmering secondary colors.

It is difficult for me to be here, to force my larynx to form these glued-together syllables already put forward by so many smooth talkers, these sinuous phrases that can argue a cause and its contrary, thesis and antithesis, with equal vigor. For my part, I prefer to hiss, as I thread my way between roots and vines, so that none may misunderstand the meaning of my message. But it seems to me that I can't use your language without becoming specious, hypocritical, manipulative—it seems to me that untruth is inherent in its very principles. Etymology supports me on this: your words hide what they really mean, or else they have forgotten it, they have mutated, adapted ceaselessly as if they had no truth to preserve or defend. One by one they have repudiated their every ephemeral meaning in order to shore up, now and then, a new imposture.

How could I ever make myself heard in such conditions, and what will you understand? Perhaps I should have stuck to my first idea. Yes, surely I should have come here simply to appear before you, ladies, gentlemen, and howl bloody murder.

An Overwhelming Success

When I began laying out my imaginary museum, I could scarcely anticipate the indignities and misadventures it would cause. Given such foreknowledge, I would almost certainly have called off the plan before even laying the first stone—an expression to be understood here in its figurative sense, needless to say, the primary characteristic of imaginary museums being that they can be erected without the mobilizing or immobilizing of any construction equipment. I completely neglected the architecture of my museum, anyway, occupied as I was solely with assembling my collections. This was a mistake. I realized it much too late.

About my collections. With the exception of Egyptian, Greek, and Roman antiquities, in which I have little interest, I used a broad brush, so to speak. I spared no expense. I let my tastes and preferences guide me, of course, while also making an effort to be comprehensive. I devoted a room to tribal art. All the Renaissance masters were represented in the room dedicated to Italian painting. Spanish painting had its gallery, as did Flemish painting. I decked my mental gallery walls with canvases representing all the schools, all the movements of modern art. And I'm not one of those people who are so narrow-minded that their imaginary museum fits inside a hallway, who believe there are no more creators today: contemporary art was allotted its space, where I envisioned mostly temporary exhibitions (since the contemporary doesn't tend to last very long).

It took me some time, as you might imagine, to get the works together. Even if questions of logistics, insurance, and transport are greatly simplified for the curator of an imaginary museum, he is nonetheless anything but exempt from organizational concerns.

At last everything was ready, and I was eagerly looking forward to one of those secret parties of the mind to commemorate the opening—something intimate, a solitary pleasure, an interior ecstasy. I opened a good bottle of wine (I also have a well-stocked imaginary wine cellar), I chose the best armchair from my parlor, I dimmed the lights, and I closed my eyes. And then. And then . . . And then! Damn it all to hell, a queue several dozen yards long stretched out before the entrance to my imaginary museum!

How had word gotten out? I'd let no one in on my secret. Had I talked in my sleep, allowing one or another of my lovers to spread the news from pillow to pillow around town? Had I been betrayed by one of the drunken jags I methodically undertake in local bars to kill the few hours I don't devote to contemplation? Do the bottles from which we chug drink our words as well? Whatever the case, there they were, hundreds of visitors, lined up before the entrance to my imaginary museum.

I opened the doors—what else could I do? I couldn't risk a riot or a stampede. (Think, after all, of the universal masterworks gathered inside. The *Mona Lisa*? I had managed, not without a great deal of persistence and elaborate security provisions, to obtain from the Louvre an exceptional loan of the *Mona Lisa*.)

I opened the doors, my repose ended, and my troubles began. My mind was literally overtaken. All the tour operators had put my museum on their itineraries. In their haste, a number of American tourists even skipped Florence and Amsterdam so as not to miss this newly indispensable fixture on the European cultural circuit. (This was understandable; the primary works from the Uffizi and the Rijksmuseum were now displayed on my top floor.) The first Japanese tour buses had already begun parking diagonally around my buzzing skull. I had forbidden photography, but there was no shortage of violators, and the flickers from their flashbulbs fried my brain.

Such disruptions! Though I have always had a very calm inner life, though I learned from my old Chinese master to make a void in my mind to accommodate the serene dream of a world freed of the self, I was being invaded. People flowed in tightly packed rows through my imaginary museum from morning to evening, and late-night visits were even arranged against my will. Impossible to sleep a wink.

I had to take immediate action. Of course I considered secretly moving my museum, but to where? What place would be safe? The impossibility of this is obvious enough, I think, that I needn't say more. Instead, I fixed strict, nonnegotiable visiting hours: my imaginary museum would henceforth be open every day except Tuesdays, from 9 a.m. to 6 p.m. (Need I add that no discount was offered to military service members?) I was able to rigorously maintain these rules and keep all access points locked the rest of the time, thanks to my long-standing and time-tested practice of repression.

I also hired imaginary guards, from among the ghosts of my past and the blurry silhouettes that people my dreams, to watch over my collections during visiting hours. I dressed them in handsome starched uniforms to stiffen them up, which allowed the majority of them to successfully stay upright. It was obviously difficult, however, to demand their vigilance at every moment. Children slid on the parquet floors, causing me atrocious (and anything but imaginary!) migraines. There were also some lamentable damages: an Egon Schiele nude attacked with acid, a Michelangelo marble attacked with a chisel. And I could barely tolerate the incessant sketching of the art school students and other more or less talented hobbyists who camped out in my brain from morning to night, their approximate figure drawings blurring my own clear representations.

And finally, one morning, opening the doors to let the visitors in, I found my museum ravaged, empty frames scattered across the floor. All the canvases had been neatly cut out and stolen. Nothing was left on the walls but a few drawings by my children and three or four of my own pieces that I had boldly mixed in with my collections. No doubt I should have installed an alarm system—and yet I've come to think that this omission was no accident, that in making it I was inviting the thieves to help themselves in the hopes of regaining, once they'd come and gone, some inner peace: a peace without images, without shapes or colors, the blessed primordial emptiness of those uncreated worlds where everything remains to be done.

Faldoni

—Excuse me, sir, would you take our picture? This said as they hand him the camera.

—No.

Such is Faldoni.

Then he resumes his interrupted motion. His left hand grips the iron rod. His right vigorously operates the crank. What do you think he's doing? Faldoni: what would you have him be doing? He's lowering his iron curtain. Putting his heart and soul into it. Not the type to go in for an electric shutter, Faldoni. He insists on executing the maneuver himself. All this iron he's extracting from the sky, it's prodigious.

Later, we see him again. Faldoni is walking in small steps on the square, not far from his shop. He has a white plastic bag in his hand. We wonder what's inside. Faldoni is wearing a silk sweater, a bright chestnut color but somewhat faded: beige, to be perfectly frank. And dark pants, a bit baggy, that pleat above his shoes. He's a rather corpulent man, Faldoni. A rather corpulent little man. The sweater clings tightly to his figure, to his preadolescent breasts, his excessive belly. His navel pokes out in relief too, surprisingly. His head is that of a Great Dane. There is a certain placidity to Faldoni.

He wears glasses with a fine gilded frame. But the lenses are lightly tinted. He has genuine jowls. Get an eyeful of this buffoon.

Faldoni has stopped here, just in front of us. We'd put him in his sixties. He's probably younger than that but he looks older. Sixty is a good median. Brown hair graying, sparse, combed back, smoothed over his skull. Is there a Mrs. Faldoni? It looks as if he's waiting for someone. Poor Mrs. Faldoni!

A flabby statue in the middle of the square, Faldoni. From where he stands, he can see his shop. Double display windows, one on either side of the door. Double iron curtain. Chez Faldoni. A tourist approaches to ask him the time. But Faldoni's hands are in his pockets. And couldn't the tourist have had a watch? Such is Faldoni.

The plastic bag dangling from his wrist hangs down his leg. It looks heavy, this plastic bag, which is white. Heavy and quite full. What's inside? Not caring won't get us anywhere. Will we make a character of Faldoni? The wrinkles that begin at the corners of his mouth extend the malevolent arc of his lips. He is a displeased character. Plump and displeased. His shoes are big and dark, with no other characteristics. The elementary shoe. The first notion of the biped. Just a pedestal for Faldoni.

No adjective could be less opportune to qualify this character than *stylish*. *Elegant* would also clash rudely with his outfit. The crew neck of his beige sweater reveals the collar of a blue shirt and the knot of a black necktie. Faldoni!

The curve of his skull begins at the superciliary arches. The forehead doesn't put up much of a fight. The nose is strong and snubby at once. An upturned spud. All of this is not very happy. We assume Faldoni's appearance barely preoccupies him. His charm lies elsewhere. We don't know where.

Concern for his appearance is one fewer concern for Faldoni, who is a concerned man. We must not be misled on this point by his placidity. Faldoni is no stranger to worry and doubt. He shifts his weight, to one leg and then to the other. Imperceptibly, Faldoni is dancing. We restrain ourselves from applauding. (No use tying our hands behind our backs.) It's a sign of discomfort, though, or of anxiety. Something is bothering the fat man. A black worm gnaws at the fruit that is Faldoni.

Why this bitter grimace? His face sags like a body whose knees have given out, followed by the shoulders. Faldoni is ponderous. He's heavy. He's ballasted, and not just by his weight. From time to time he stirs. He takes a step to the side. He moves in slow motion. He slips in glue. There is unmistakably, in Faldoni, something of the gastropod.

His hands have come out of his pockets. The plastic bag rests against his stomach, with its mysterious contents. We can't help advancing some hypotheses. What is Faldoni looking at? Another subject of interrogation and debate. His darkened glasses reflect the metal shutters of his shop. This is how he sees himself, perhaps. Contemplative with dead eyes.

Faldoni calls to mind Loqueteau, a bit, for those who knew him. Loqueteau had the same general bearing as Faldoni. But on one hand, Loqueteau has been dead for a good fifteen years now. On the other hand, Loqueteau was the salt of the earth. Which in no way diminishes their resemblance. Whoever knew Loqueteau, seeing Faldoni, will recall Loqueteau. But how many of us will there be in this situation, who knew Loqueteau and meet Faldoni? Loqueteau, like Faldoni, was not very energetic. Only great travelers will have chanced to cross Loqueteau's path and then Faldoni's. The two paths, of sand and of mud, leading to these two bog-bound specimens. But how to not prefer Loqueteau? Faldoni inspires immediate antipathy. It is a gift, a grace. It takes no doing of his own.

A couple of foreign tourists come to him on the square. The man unfolds a map under his eyes. With broad gestures, the woman tries to make herself understood. It's clear they're asking for directions. Evidently they know nothing of Faldoni. In a similar situation Loqueteau would have offered his assistance with haste and compunction and bashfulness, of this we can be sure. For those still seeking more differences between Loqueteau and Faldoni, there's one. Loqueteau was the very picture of goodness; gruff, sheepish, a bit stupid. Faldoni doesn't bother to answer the little couple. As if he hasn't seen them. Couldn't they have just learned the language, these two? Plus Faldoni doesn't like being mistaken for the tourism office. He turns his head away slowly. Here is his profile. At least we're in no danger of seeing the other side, so long as this one is on display. But that's the sole satisfaction this spectacle provides.

Do his friends call him Faldo? His friends! Why not his lovers too?!

This is Faldoni we're talking about: no friends, no lovers. Poor Mrs. Faldoni!

What is he thinking about? Because Faldoni is thinking. He's thinking about something, anyway. There's a thought darkening that face, obstructing it. But is it a torment or a dream? There is ultimately plenty of mystery in Faldoni. It could be that it's merely thickness: the opacity of a dirty window. That bag, though. There's definitely something in it.

At once massive, static, and blurry, cloudy: Faldoni. We wouldn't be surprised to see him spread and permeate. But he's standing there, upright, motionless as a mile marker. His face barely changes its expression, frozen in disgust and refusal.

—No.

Faldoni has spoken.

His beige sweater really is too tight for him. Did he buy it too small? Did he fatten inside it? We watch Faldoni and no end of new questions come to us. He swivels at his hips: here he is again in front of his boutique. We don't dare think he's there on duty, as a sentinel, keeping watch. As though the full-slatted double iron curtain doesn't defend it sufficiently. Against what? Against the undesired intrusions of clients, for one thing. It's undeniable, Faldoni approaches a certain form of perfection. Faldoni, to the tips of his podgy fingers, and better than Loqueteau, embodies Faldoni. All perfection is fragile; it's always just *this* close. One word too many and it all falls apart.

From the end of his arm dangles the white plastic bag whose folds conceal the shape it contains. We can't say the same for Faldoni in his beige sweater. We can say the opposite, and truthfully. The beige sweater hides nothing of Faldoni. Which is regrettable. This beige or beigeish silk could be Faldoni's own mane. His dull, short-cropped fleece. Nothing to shear off to clothe the naked. Not a strand to lend the builders of nests. Not that it's easy to imagine Faldoni as an angora. Faldoni as a merino, vicuña, or mink: unlikely. The beige sweater is a girdle, a sheath, a special limited-edition Faldoni slipcase. The beige sweater is Faldoni's mossy bark. The beige sweater is Faldoni's fuzzy hide. A beige sweater that must be all distended. Shapeless. Absurd without Faldoni inside it. And what's become of Loqueteau's sweaters, now that he's dead? It's a good question. It would be a boon for Faldoni to lay his hands on that wardrobe. And, for Loqueteau's beige or beigeish sweaters, something like a second life.

Faldoni lifts his chin slightly. We won't go so far as to say he's inhaling the good, fine sun. Why not also crouch down to breathe in a little floweret? Faldoni! A fat gentleman, hands deep in his pockets again. A flabby statue in the style of Loqueteau. Hostile. Poor Mrs. Faldoni! We don't know if she exists, but how we pity her! We wish we could smile kindly at her. And so we wonder how Faldoni would react if one of us were to calmly approach and embrace him. Lay a surprise kiss on his jowl. Give him a skritch on the nape of his neck. Slip a gentle hand under the beige sweater. Any volunteers?

It should be noted that our scrutiny hardly bothers Faldoni. He persists in his being with an astonishing lack of shame. Our eyes would obliterate him if they could, but they don't even irritate him as much as a swarm of flies would. He'd puff up instead, Faldoni. It's an understatement to say he doesn't crumble. He obstructs. He's all we see.

Loqueteau was surely less compact, less opaque than Faldoni. Loqueteau was more like whipped cream, cheese soufflé: there was wind and flight in him. But he didn't leave the ground. There was also something of Faldoni there, enough to ballast him. But Loqueteau was a pool of limpid water compared to Faldoni. You could see the bottom. He had no plastic bag. Even just that. He wasn't a secretive man. Stumpy, yes. But practically bare, practically naked. Offered up entirely to our gaze. Pure ivory. He hid nothing from us.

What do we truly know of Faldoni? Would we say, for instance, that he's an honest shopkeeper? That would be committing to a lot. But he's hung out his shingle, to that we can attest. His name stretches across the pediment of his shop. We wonder all the same whether it's not dirty money from some scheme or other that he's stuffed in his bag. We'd hardly be shocked to see it pass surreptitiously into the hands of a gray-cheeked accomplice. Let us remain vigilant. Or perhaps it's Mrs. Faldoni's head. Poor Mrs. Faldoni's head. Bagged. Whereas to our knowledge there was never a Mrs. Loqueteau. Poor Mrs. Loqueteau. She would have been so happy with sweet Loqueteau.

Why did Faldoni kill his wife? Ah! Will we ever penetrate the enigma that is Faldoni! What eye could be so shrewd as to bore to the heart of this adipose mass? And what eye so patient as to get to the bottom of it? What eye would consent to give him all its blue, all its black, and open thenceforth for nothing but him?

Sometimes we believe we're holding Faldoni in place, and then Bam! He disappears. Such an imposing character, who'd have imagined? A will-o'-the-wisp! Dugong, manatee, sperm whale, hippopotamus, or walrus, Faldoni. These are the comparisons that occur to us, preceded by a strong sound of lapping waves. He's an eel! All his fat is merely tallow. Faldoni slips between our fingers. His whole being imperceptibly sloshes, incessantly swerves. Flighty Faldoni, elusive Faldoni. Water, sand, an idle thought, Faldoni, a dream. We'll wake up flushed and sweating, choked by the bedsheets.

Like a ball of yarn under a cat's paw. Faldoni. Two hundred forty-six pounds of beige or beigeish silk on parade. Loqueteau, you could shake his hand. The sweat at the joints of his knuckles was a good strong glue. You could hold on to him. The hard part was getting free again afterward.

Oh! How we wish we could pummel this big fatty with our fists! Faldoni! Who's now passing himself off as smoke, an evanescent mist. Look at that roguish air. That weary haughtiness. That Great Dane face. We'd like to pummel that belly with our fists. Aim for Faldoni's liver, Faldoni's spleen, Faldoni's stomach. Punch, punch, with the left, with the right, into Faldoni's fat. Destroy this character. Flay him. Burst him open like a goatskin gourd. Crush this piece of crap. Kill Faldoni. He definitely killed his wife. A simple working hypothesis, fine. But the bag. There's still the bag. Is the bag not a clue?

Faldoni takes a few steps. Good of you to distract us a bit. Then he returns to his spot. That's it for the action.

Loqueteau moved around more. Loqueteau wasn't exactly a live spectacle either, mind you. There was flabbiness in Loqueteau too, a laziness of the muscles and bones. The mind perpetually aware of the body's weight. But sometimes Loqueteau's eyelid would unmistakably wink. So often we'd see a smile knife its way through the octopus flesh of his lips. We'd see his fat fingers play with a pencil. Loqueteau was endowed with mobility. Whereas Faldoni could just as well roll, drawn down by a slope. Or stirred by a sudden gust of wind. Then, the momentum broken, return to his initial position here in front of us.

This man was born of woman. We barely believe it. Was a child. Skipped to and fro. Faldoni! Nonsense! Faldoni has always been here. This is his place. He's planted too firmly to be just passing through. In this place in space, there is Faldoni.

An accident on the surface of the globe, like a mountain, Faldoni. He won't age, won't wrinkle, won't wither. His bones are not the kind to wind up under the earth. They're enshrouded already, scattered uselessly inside Faldoni. No, not a mountain: to speak of mountains is to dream of peaks and chamois, to touch the sky: we lose ourselves in such altitudes. *Heap* says all there is to be said about Faldoni. *Heap* names the thing. Faldoni? A heap. Wide in the hips and the belly, narrow in the shoulders, topped off with a sagging hat, Faldoni. A collapsed pyramid. A heap, but a coherent heap, a homogenous heap, not a heap of miscellaneous goods, various things. A heap of Faldoni. It is Faldoni heaped up there.

For here is Faldoni: covered in Faldoni, lined with Faldoni, stuffed with Faldoni. No other matter, no other material: 100 percent Faldoni. We could swear his pockets, too, are full of Faldoni. He was a clay or a paste or a glue whose source has since dried up, the vein spent. Faldoni soaked it up, to the last drop of the geological stratum, to become Faldoni. We wring our hands to think of all the useful things that could have been made from this soft and ductile material. We weep in silence. Imagine one who confiscated rubber. It's pitiful, decidedly. There was enough there to make the town dance. Now here we are with this fat gentleman. This gently nodding elephant.

Suddenly we know why we've been dragging this quiver around since childhood. We understand why we taught ourselves to throw knives every night in our dreams. And why we've never missed a single swordsmanship class, a single tiger defense training. Something in us knew. One day there would be Faldoni in front of us. One day it would be our big moment. And sure enough. We felt it coming, yes. Monsieur was announced. He didn't have to surge up all of a sudden. He was here.

We opened our eyes and he was there. Faldoni in person. Not even Loqueteau. Faldoni. He was there the way an armoire is there. Inevitable. Crammed full of Faldoni, stitched up with Faldoni. Filled to the gills with Faldoni. For whom, all of this Faldoni? For Faldoni! And for whom, Faldoni? Woe unto us!

We didn't ask for this. We'd rather have two Loqueteaus than one Faldoni. We should be able to live with two Loqueteaus here in front of us. We can't imagine such a thing being possible for very long with a Faldoni. We'd rather have two Loqueteaus in thick gray velvet than one beige-knit Faldoni. Rather have three, four Loqueteaus. A thousand Loqueteaus, fine, fine, so long as you spare us Faldoni and his white plastic bag.

He won't go on his own. He takes a few steps from time to time, as though to give us hope. Then he comes back to plant himself here in front of us. Here's one of his secrets: his two legs are four paws.

In truth, it looks to us now as if Faldoni is spilling out of Faldoni. No eruption and no flood, however. Instead an oozing, a coulis of Faldoni. An exudation of his entire body. Faldoni is beading like a bead of sweat on the skin of Faldoni, on the silk of Faldoni. Nothing better will ever emerge from this man. It would be terribly naive of us, in fact, to expect anything else. It is a permanent suppuration. Will Faldoni finally empty himself of Faldoni? Is he purging himself of himself?

Dream on, my friends. Faldoni is secreting Faldoni. Faldoni is slapping himself on the back with congratulations for being Faldoni. And laying it on thick. Faldoni is embodying the joy of being Faldoni. The glory of being Faldoni. The pleasure of being Faldoni. His whole person says, I am Faldoni, and says only that. Has never said anything else. Just repeats it endlessly, without interruption, without exhaustion, infinitely.

Faldoni

Faldoni Faldoni

Faldoni Faldoni Faldoni

Faldoni Faldoni

Faldoni   Faldoni

Someone in this world exults in being Faldoni. As it turns out, that someone is Faldoni. Which doesn't do much for us. Here in front of us Faldoni is puffing and preening. He purrs with pleasure. Do you realize? It is he, it is Faldoni! He's dreaming of a cow's tongue. Wide as a hand and long as an arm. To lick himself all over with, on his every surface. And in the creases, the folds, in the holes. Faldoni dreams of sucking himself like a bonbon, of rolling around in his saliva. Of knowing the moist and warm caress of his mouth, the cradle of his mucus. We assume Faldoni is still greedy for Faldoni. Never satisfied, never sated. Faldoni. Always hungry for Faldoni.

Faldoni ate Faldoni in a single bite. Like the serpent ate the rat. Swallowed whole, Faldoni, giving Faldoni his shape. Alas! But here we detect something resembling, perhaps, a regret. Faldoni rues his voraciousness. He wouldn't act that way today. He's become more of a gourmet. Each day, a new morsel of Faldoni. An aiguillette of Faldoni. Chewed at length, pressed between the tongue and the palate to express all its juices, a little diced cube of Faldoni. Slice after slice, filet after filet, fiber after fiber, making this exquisite taste last as long as his life itself. This is how Faldoni, today, would savor Faldoni.

Let us make no mistake, there is still passion in him. No question of raiding the banquet with a periwinkle pick and a demitasse spoon. Faldoni didn't let those horrible little pointed teeth grow in for nothing. How readily he'd sink them into the fat of his thigh! And how he'd rip into his flanks! How he'd devour his paunch! And how round his calves are!

Faldoni nurtures a visible passion for Faldoni. Faldoni adores Faldoni. Faldoni would never have loved Loqueteau the way he loves Faldoni, for instance. He's his little Faldoni, his dear Faldoni, his sweet sugar Faldoni. In his private moments, Faldoni no doubt calls himself my chickadee, my duckling. He gives himself pet names like Puss, like Baby. Like Faldo-Faldo.

He never takes his eyes off his shop for long. But it's because he doesn't know how to point them where he wants. Because he can no longer look anywhere but into himself. Faldoni: nothing fascinates him more than the spectacle of Faldoni. To be physically unable to see his own interior is a genuine source of suffering for Faldoni. A wrenching. Something atrocious. It's like a grief, a separation. It's like being deprived, a bit, of Faldoni. We can't even fathom it. How happily Faldoni would live in contemplation of Faldoni's organs. How dearly he would pay for a glance at the lungs, the liver, the stomach and spleen of Faldoni. But he's reduced to guessing, like the other observers, at the hypertrophied, tubercular volumes budding under the beige silk. Unlike us, however, he has the option of tracing its contours with the flat of his hand. Happy man. He does not deny himself this pleasure. He palpates them with his fingertips, he masturbates them. He pats them like the cheeks of a child.

But Faldoni would rather be in our place. Our gaze embracing his person. Or let us say rather that our gaze encompasses him. (He doesn't all fit.) With pleasure, with pleasure, we would give him our spot. But then we'd find ourselves occupying his. Which would still be, for us, an unobstructed view of Faldoni. Ah, despair is never far off.

Pigeons stroll on the square around Faldoni. They resemble him. They're from the same family of oafs, lumberers, galoots. More gastropodal than the gastropod. We've seen snails and slugs on spindly stalks.

Faldoni quickly opens his white plastic bag, just a crack. He confirms the presence of an object inside. He seems reassured. Poor Mrs. Faldoni! We're sure of it, we're not fooled by this banal white plastic bag, Faldoni is hiding something from us. And something else, too: what is there behind Faldoni? We must have seen what he's hiding from us now. It was so long ago. A monument? An ocean? The cloudless horizon? We don't remember. Faldoni is the only landscape. He is to the left, he is to the right, he is at the center of it all. Sometimes, on top of it all, he smiles a satisfied little smile.

Loqueteau wasn't so invasive. No question, Loqueteau took up space. It also happened now and then that Loqueteau would block our view. Leaving us only the sky. We felt a tender, mocking compassion for Loqueteau. We laughed amongst ourselves at the excessive protuberance of the genital apparatus in his pants. When they autopsy his corpse, quipped Pommard, they'll find a bone right there. Quite frightening. In this respect, Faldoni has a lesser impact. His underpants are wide, his protuberant belly gets in the way. We don't see much. Must we dread the existence of progeny, though? A population of young Faldonis, in its turn procreating new Faldonis—Could such a thing be possible? Boys and girls—girls!—of all ages, made in the image of their father. Poor Mrs. Faldoni!

And yet there's no room for two Faldonis. No, we don't see how another Faldoni could stand there next to Faldoni. Should we rejoice? Two Faldonis could turn against each other. A fratricidal war to sort things out for us. They'd mutually weaken each other. They'd kill each other, maybe. Imagine the blanket of sweetness and joy we could lay over the bodies of two Faldonis on the tiled floor. Unless of course they didn't fight but instead fused into one. Suctioned together at the flanks. Unless of course they united. Faldoni plus Faldoni. Double buttocks of Faldoni, double belly of Faldoni, double head of Faldoni. Double double fat. Double malediction. Mercy!

The police do nothing, the army does nothing, the church does nothing, medical science does nothing. Lumberjacks do nothing, garbagemen do nothing, ditch diggers do nothing. Faldoni remains, undecaying, rotproof. Here, in front of us. Sometimes the flabby statue trembles slightly on its base. An internal laugh, perhaps, makes it move. Faldoni wriggles imperceptibly. Is he mocking us? Or is he rather delighting at the thought of what's in his plastic bag? Victuals for his dinner, or something else? What? Pastries? Hardware? Lingerie? A thought, friends, for Mrs. Faldoni.

Faldoni attracts, aspirates, absorbs all that's around. If we got up to leave, we might get sucked up. Assimilated. Wind up in the amalgam. It's a risk we can't bring ourselves to take, is it not? At the thought of such a horrid intermixture, everything inside us retracts. Revolts. Better to stay here forever. Without moving, until the bitter end. Before us, Faldoni.

Or is this the bitter end already? Have we reached the end? Is it because we're at the end that there is Faldoni? Is there nothing behind, nothing after Faldoni? For the first time, our gaze meets his. We weren't wrong. A cruel smile tells us so. We don't dare turn around. Behind us too, already, there is Faldoni. No more steppes, no more desert without Faldoni. Close our eyes? Perish the thought! To do so would be to invite him under our eyelids. The entire mass of Faldoni settling into our skulls. Better to look him in the face. And keep quiet. How did we not think of that earlier? Maybe Faldoni will disappear if we keep quiet? We have to try everything. Let us try.

To Live Hidden
in Clear Water

See, likewise, the goldfish behind the glass wall of his aquarium. He seldom moves, but he's always there. He can be counted on, or in any case his presence can. Sometimes he shows his right profile, other times his left profile. Not so fascinating a spectacle, you say? And yet, curiously, we don't get tired of it. He might hide behind his rock; he might suction himself to the wall. Maybe he'll nibble at a bit of his seaweed. Today he's remained practically motionless. But yesterday—did you *see* him yesterday?—he wouldn't stay still, so brisk, so quick that his shape dissolved into sheer speed; all you could see was a red-orange line, like a firework rocket. Impossible to say where the head was, or the tail. We guessed at random. My opinion is that he shattered his personal record, maybe that of his whole weight class too. On still a different day, his stroke zigzagged him from one corner of the volume of water to the other. In the calm of the living room, only he was agitated. In truth, he was the one who caused the chaos. And so the disorder spread to the things around him. We watched with a suspicious eye. Were we going to have to learn to mistrust goldfish too? A strange creature, really, bearing a contradictory resemblance to both a flame and a bar of soap. Doesn't he seem to be only just barely keeping his blood between his two sides, beneath his scales? Doesn't he seem to be life laid utterly bare, no more than its essential palpitation, its simplest expression? For that matter, is this water actually his element? Doesn't he really move through time instead? With ease, some days, even with grace; everything yields to him, as though the tide were parting to let him pass, each second vindicating him. Ah, but then on other days it's a different story altogether! Those days he seems to be a prisoner in a block of amber or resin. Each second seals him in its capsule. The goldfish has no memory, they say, but the instant bears down on him, dense with the entirety of the past; no longer knowing when his life began, he feels the weight of numberless centuries. You'd like to lend him a hand. But try lending a goldfish a hand! He'll explode between your fingers like an overripe plum. Better to wait with him: better to wait for it to pass. And indeed, suddenly, something comes unstuck and he's found an exit. He's off again. From a certain angle of the living room, who can say why, the aquarium's glass produces a magnifying effect and our goldfish—a modest apartment carp—grows to massive proportions. All of a sudden he's an underwater monster. We tremble from our encoignure. It would seem he also changes according to our mood, to our point of view. Though it would be too much to project everything onto him, not least our own size! For, conversely, if we bend at the knee, he also shrinks, narrows. Or does he melt? We manage, in any case, to make him disappear. Nothing left but his water, a bit murky. And then, if we look from an angle, across the sharp corner of the aquarium: he's doubled! Two goldfish! A companion for him at last, a fiancée. But no! How painful these optical effects are, how misleading! If our eye plays tricks on us too, how can we ever hope to draw closer to reality? We must admit it, then, once and for all:

our goldfish is alone. He is publicly manifesting an experience of solitude. He has opted, courageously, for the utmost transparency. He hides nothing. A few ulterior motives, perhaps. We can track him hour by hour, minute by minute. We can watch him sleep. Even the most intimate necessities of nature he offers to us as a spectacle—though maybe in those cases he's counting on our discretion, our modesty. How wrong he is about us! Or maybe his exhibitionism is a sly snare for our voyeurism? For we must never forget this: it is impossible to know the face of a goldfish. It's too thin. It could just as well be a blade, or a horse. He never exposes himself any way but in profile—but what does he do with the other side? His other profile, during this time, what's it doing? What's it hiding? Could this transparency be a red herring? Could he be taking us for a ride, on a boat? It's so obvious it's blinding. Nor can we forget that he's a descendant of the carp, that habitué of muds and silts. We can change his water all we like, we can clean the glass wall of the aquarium with a squeegee, a chamois cloth; he'll always find a way to conceal from our observation that which he intends to hide. He shows us so much sincerity that we never see the bottom, in which sense his sincerity is not so different, finally, from silt. And then, drowned alive in a solid body of water, submerged in that element in which we'd suffocate, can we tell ourselves he's happy here, with us, in this living room, that he's one of our number? The glass seems thin, but if we were to break it in an effort to establish a warmer, friendlier rapport, our solicitude would surely be deadly. In sum, this goldfish is as distant from us as if he lived in the deepest depths of the water, among the blind and pallid creatures of the ocean floor. And yet we're not dreaming: sometimes, he gives us a sign. And he comes to the surface as soon as we give him his daily ration of daphnia. His indifference is a lie. He needs us. Maybe he even sees our living room as a decorative feature of his aquarium. Our comings and goings distract him from his melancholy. We're the characters who people his dreams. His mouth forms little bubbles that detach soundlessly from his lips . . . could he be trying to tell us something?

But what?

The Door

Is there anything more idiotic than a door? The very idea could only have come from a mind that was itself open too wide, if not downright unhinged. For either the door provides passage at a point in space where there was formerly nothing to impede free circulation, thus standing guard over it completely uselessly, or it forbids access to this or that place by closing it off, but in that case it's not enough, because as soon as it's installed you have to put high walls around it, which means arranging a tiresome cartage of stones and beams, an entire industry of the most exhausting sort, followed by a superhuman labor that hurls the masons up to vertiginous heights on their makeshift scaffolding while the mind-numbing music of the spheres, captured on their transistor radios, resonates all around. Then the carpenters and roofers wrenched from the earth's gravitational pull urgently have to build themselves a damp slate slide to get back to the ground, a black-diamond ski run that leads them down from the mountain, not without contusions and traumas of which quadriplegia is the least common multiple.

All this because of the door. And once it's finally hung on its hinges, after we've swept away the knucklebones and fingertips littering the threshold and turned the key twice in the lock, we immediately have to carve a cat flap into the bottom because Puss is outside meowing loud enough to wake the dead, hungry and muddy and dreadfully leprous, which cat flap will have to be enlarged further because the poor thing has been mounted by all the neighborhood's unchipped tomcats and now she's so bursting with babies that she has to brood her eggs in two saddlebags dangling from her flanks.

And now that we've started sawing into the wooden board, that's not all: we also have to cut a slit in the center, lest our mail remain delivery pending, not to mention an eyehole or a peephole so we can get a look at the intruder who comes knocking at all hours before we open up, which we have to do before we can send him away with a boot to the backside.

Honestly, I can't think of anything to say in favor of the door, which we sometimes push and sometimes pull, inevitably having to try twice because some strange malediction systematically ensures that our first guess is the wrong one. And yes, granted, we can also slam it forcefully to express our discontent—but what's wrong with the good old-fashioned slap? Last time I checked, it wasn't just for the one-armed—plus it has the advantage of not requiring a visit from a carpenter first. The door is an aberration, justified by nothing.

But then what to do? I have the answer, friends: take the doors down! Let us unhinge them—better them than us, after all. We'll make our doors into sleds, rafts on which to set off and discover the world instead of cloistering ourselves in our rancid interiors with the domesticated cockroach and the germinated potato. Thus will we go forth, through space open to all manner of adventure, free as the air beneath the stars, moved to our innermost depths by the newfound gentleness of things.

The Museum Visit (2)

Modern man is more predictable than the return of the full moon at the end of the month. Take a quick poll of a museum's visitors and you'll have your confirmation: they're all there to see the works on display and admire the collections. What feeble imaginations! A veritable troop of Panurge's sheep, crowding into those rooms. Are we all yoked to one another with iron rings, like mine carts? I'm not so suggestible, and if I can sometimes be seen at church of a Sunday morning I'm certainly not there to pray to God: rather, I'm taking advantage of the organ music and the incense to contemplate myself with a delicious self-satisfaction.

So it goes for museums too. It's not a taste for painting that unstintingly leads my feet to their doors. When I see men and women of all ages parade by self-importantly with their hands behind their backs, planted before the paintings, right in front, so smugly sure of their noble standing, breathing as deeply as if they were filling their lungs with the airs of Flanders or Tuscany, I can't resist an ironic smile—even as anguish enters deep into my soul.

What, then, you ask, brings me to museums of fine art? Why am I so often the first to arrive and the last to leave? My stance would doubtless reveal my secret to the observer, if he didn't inexplicably prefer to focus his attention on the portraits and landscapes of the Flemish or Italian masters. Look at me, though: I stand not in front of these painted canvases, whose subjects leave me as indifferent as their styles, but always to the side, at an angle, slightly off-center: I have come for the frames. Frames—now that's something else. Speak to me of frames! Here is the highest expression of art, where it finally reaches its full potential. It's not lost in the anecdotage of the religious or the bucolic, not blinded by showy obviousness: it seeks the truth in the margins. Those four lengths of wood bind the world tightly, its rivers and its mountains and all the madness of humankind. Tooled with adzes, with gouges, with scissors, richly ornamented with scrolls or garlands of acanthus leaves, laurel leaves, foliage in flower, palmettos, gadroons, shells, bunches of grapes, then gilded as though by the sun itself, they utterly eclipse, for the aficionado, the banal little scenes they enclose.

The experiment is easily done. Equip yourself with such a frame, the size of your torso, and stroll through the city, careful to keep yourself centered, and you'll see gawkers flock, you'll be pointed out and pointed at. Everywhere you will awaken curiosity. Tourists will take your photograph; some will even beg to be immortalized next to you. It's not out of the question that deeply moved passersby will slip a few coins into your pocket. And all of this, mind you, even if you're ordinarily the invisible type, accustomed to the scorn or the indifference of the crowd, rudely jostled on sidewalks and universally taken for a dreary embodiment of insignificance. Suddenly women who never gave you the time of day will shoot you their most ardent come-hither looks, then write their phone numbers in lipstick on your forehead. Here you are now, painted handsome as a marquis, all the ladies of the court rushing to your side.

Conversely, a painting suddenly deprived of its frame loses all appeal, much as the spectacle that titillates us through the keyhole bores us once the door opens to invite us in. I'll say it without hesitation: it's the frame that makes the painting. Without it, the still life turns back to bric-a-brac, the vanity back to the ossuary. Without it, the seascape is no more than an ignoble blotch of dampness on the wall. Even Christ's cross aligns itself parallel to its borders. The frame makes the painting, just as the window makes the landscape. Without a window, no landscape. In the place of this landscape that so delighted the eye, a wall.

And how can we not admire the modesty of the framers? They never sign their work, never demand even a crumb of the glory that falls to those painters whose name is written on the plaque even though it's already at the bottom of the canvas, those painters who sometimes carry their self-satisfaction to the point of self-portraiture. It would be easy for the framers, master cabinetmakers that they are, to carve their profile into little medallions among the vine branches and ferns, but they're not so presumptuous. They let time carry them into oblivion, finding their life's justification in the happy knowledge of a job well done. They needed but a single paintbrush. They dipped it in golden light, leaving to the drudges and doodlers the work of brushing in the rest, adding details, applying colors, and to us all things are revealed.

Execration

He hated me with an absolute, insatiable passion. So great was his loathing that it was enough for him to catch sight of me to begin ranting and railing. If he hadn't also drooled, I believe he might have caught on fire. Hearing my name, even murmured at a distance, deep in a forest, under a rock, beside a spring, filled him with rage. He would stomp around, and woe unto those who happened to find themselves where his foot fell. It was he who one day kicked a crack in the seashell curve of this world. His hatred brooked neither respite nor repose. The tempest rumbling inside him spooked lookouts on all seven seas. I'm barely exaggerating. You could feel his entire being consumed by murderous desires. For my part, I felt nothing toward him whatsoever.

It was he who sulked and snarled.

I became accustomed to my enemy's existence. Specialists have always fascinated me. But I couldn't follow the reasons for his hatred. I felt that his insults and abuses were poorly chosen. I was hardly impervious to attack, but he inveighed against me for the wrong reasons. I decided to let him know. I made my confession. I revealed to him my true turpitudes. And the more he learned about me, of course, the greater his animosity and vengefulness grew, the bitterer the torments he summoned upon me.

It was he who got an ulcer.

I must say I appreciated his constancy and his devotion. He hated only me. There was a certain fidelity in this— the kind we often expect, in vain, from love. He despised me from morning till night, then despised me in his nightmares; he despised me unswervingly, unsofteningly. I represented, for him, all that is to be execrated. I hid none of my pettiest thoughts, none of the cowardices and betrayals of which I was guilty.

It was he who got depressed.

I relied on him entirely. I, who have never suffered overmuch from self-love, now had at my disposal this zealous servant who relieved me of the responsibility of abhorring myself. I was exempted. What relief! I was able to attend to other things, to pursue self-satisfaction to the point of abject complacency. Which abjection he denounced with vigor, cursing it to the skies. I no longer had to bother.

It was he who got cancer.

I made a point of supplying grist to his mill. I spared him none of my weaknesses, my dishonors, my dirty tricks, my fiascos. My downfall occupied his every thought. It oppressed him. All the more carefreeness for me, all the more lightness. I knew someone was there to judge me harshly.

Because that attention was already lavished on me, I had no need to demand it of myself. The court of my conscience closed the case. My analyst went to live with his mother, moved back into his childhood womb. My parish priest waited for me in his confession booth until he began to starve, deciding after a month to eat the spider. My enemy replaced them all; he replaced me myself.

It was he who blew his brains out.

Today I miss him, I miss him dearly. So sometimes I go visit his grave. I scrupulously fill him in on my infamy. I even embellish it a bit, just for his displeasure. I beg him to keep watching over me from where he is now. To send me a sign, a stroke of bad luck, a spatter of rain. I want to believe his hatred is stronger than death. I spill my successes over the stone, boasting with that false modesty that never fooled him, not even once. I like to hear the sound his body makes as it turns over in the grave, though it's getting fainter and fainter over time. The original dull thumps have given way to a little jingle of tiny bones. Thankfully my ear is sharp. Once I can no longer make out the slightest noise, it will mean his hatred for me has faded away once and for all.

And then it will be time for me to find a new enemy.

The Cold

Cold is an unpleasant sensation. Think of it what you will, but I for one am not in favor. Intellectually, for starters, I don't see why we need it, and physically too I say no. Look, it's simple: my whole body shrinks away from the idea alone, before the sensation is even felt. My glabrous skin bristles like the fur of a cat left to a pack of dogs. My sex recoils, curls up, practically invaginates itself, desperate to find some sensual pleasure in this hostile world. One thing's for sure: it won't stand, won't stretch, won't point in any direction that could even claim to be a pole. It wants nothing to do with the cold. Not breaking ice, not chopping wood for the fire.

The cold is a truly pitiful phenomenon. We chatter our teeth as if we're about to sink them into some toothsome prey—but what a meager meal the skeleton makes for the skeleton! Our lips turn blue: death has laid its finger upon them. Our clumsy hands have abandoned caresses, music, the delicate labors of sewing and writing. Sure, we can still knock out a seal with these clubs of ours, but that's about it.

We cover ourselves up. We are pitiless predators of the sheep, lying in wait on high branches and falling on it so savagely that it prefers the company of the wolf. We wear its hand-me-downs, down to the two pairs of thick socks inexplicably provided by its scrawny paws. Scratching our nails between the ears of its smooth, close-cropped head, we even pull off a little pom-pom to cap our caps.

All to no avail. The cold cuts through these woolens like a knife. And then it shears us, flays us alive. All we can do is bleat into the speech bubble of mist hitched to our lips. As for the common cold, it lies in wait, just under our noses. Snot beads in our frozen ducts. Shivering, numb down to the marrow, we feel nothing, none of the fine sensations that distinguish us from logs—like whom, in fact, we dream of the flames that will give us back our color, our crackling wit. We make fast friends with the sphinx-headed andirons in the fireplace, immobile and taciturn, our merriest pals and hardiest comrades.

So what to do? I see only one solution: heating! Let us make heat, friends, let us burn it all! This inflammable world simply yearns to catch fire. Do you think the slender matchstick—first twig of the inferno that is the future garden of Eden—will, after ravaging the forest, leave our structures wooden and the ice sheets unmoved? And then go we shall over the melted snows, over the glowing embers, over the tender ashes, into a steam bath whose dimensions are the world's, tenderized to a swoon by the newfound gentleness of things.

Moles

When he was a child, his parents' property abutted Samuel Beckett's in Ussy-sur-Marne. Nothing entertained him more than tossing moles over the wall into the writer's yard. To hear him tell it, this was even his primary pastime. Maybe his only pastime, in fact. Today he takes pride in this former neighborship, and boasts about his childish games. We hear nothing else.

When I was a child, we lived next to Samuel Beckett's house in Ussy. I used to love tossing moles into his yard.

In no way is this hard to believe. The man telling us this has shifty eyes, and his teeth are atrocious. He teaches electrical engineering at the Lycée Désiré Nisard. He enjoys it. He claims to have a good rapport with his students. But what you mainly notice is his diseased skin, those red patches on his face and hands, the desquamations, the scabs.

Chronic eczema. A rare, complicated form. I use ointments.

Not that we asked him. Beckett—that's of greater interest to us. This man lived next door to Beckett, after all. What memories does he have of him?

I used to toss moles into his yard when I was little.

So here is a man who actually lived for several years next door to Beckett, no less than that, and who has nothing better to tell us than this: he used to toss moles into his yard, over the wall, for fun.

I'd smoke them out of their tunnels. They'd come out of the ground in a daze, zigzagging blindly. Moles in the sun are so stupid! I'd knock them out with the flat side of a shovel, without killing them.

Then he would toss them over the wall, to Beckett's property: this we know. In short, this idiotic child tried to provoke one of the great geniuses of his century. And still doesn't seem to feel any shame about it today. Which might be the most amazing thing. Because he would bombard Beckett's yard with moles, to hear him tell it. And the moles laid waste to Beckett's yard. And Beckett almost certainly suffered for it.

We are in the presence of someone who deliberately caused Beckett harm and who's still bragging about it today. He's telling us because he knows we're fans of literature and of Beckett. Is he trying to impress us with his story? Or to arouse our jealousy, maybe, or our admiration? Just as one would boast of having had a long and close relationship with Beckett.

I knew Beckett well. I even tossed moles into his yard.

Only he can say as much. Who else? No one else. Not even Beckett's closest friends and loved ones had that relationship to him.

Only me.

Or is he directing against us, now, the same malice he manifested toward Beckett? Would he strike us today with the same moles that once hit Beckett? Knowing that we're fans of literature and of Beckett, does he hope to hurt us by telling us all this? Is he stealthily aiming his mole cannon at us even as we speak?

And it's true, it really is a bit painful for us to imagine the flight of the moles, lobbed like grenades, over Beckett's wall. Painful for us to see them falling on Beckett's lawn, in Beckett's flowerbeds, and immediately digging their holes. Behold, the devastation of the lush green garden where Beckett at last found peace. Behold the ruination come to Beckett's yard, where peace could once be found. Chaos has reclaimed the land, and it did not act alone. The earth is all muddled and upended in Beckett's yard. Look at it, as pitiful as a battlefield. The grass no longer grows. The earth is covered in lumps in Beckett's yard. And this little brat, this cretin, is still tickled by it. And his smile bares his teeth, all of them wretched, with the exception of three or four that are missing.

I'd grab the unconscious moles by the scruff of their neck, and then oop! I'd throw them over the wall, into the yard of Samuel Beckett, the writer.

Or maybe he doesn't mean to hurt us at all. Maybe he's just making a spectacle of his stupidity. Which is ample! Never has so much of it been seen in the possession of a single owner.

On one side of the wall, Beckett, in the painful throes of his fierce, estimable oeuvre. On the other side of the wall the little brat, chasing moles, determined to disturb him. And who's still bragging about it today.

They were little brown moles, almost black, with smooth skin, with pink hands and feet, very small. Who would sail over the wall like grenades. Who would quickly bury themselves in Beckett's flowerbeds, under his lawn, and cause all manner of damage. Sometimes a tiny panicked head would pop up, at the top of one molehill or another, like Winnie in *Happy Days*.

Those really were the days. I was a playful kid, mischievous, always making fun. A real little devil, my mother said.

A real little brat. A face made for the fist. A butt for the boot. Even today. You'd gladly push just out of his reach the ointments that soothe his itches. You'd hurl the tube over to the other side of the wall.

He lived next door to Beckett and couldn't find anything better to do than toss moles into his yard. Instead of bringing him blackberries, mushrooms, walnuts. Instead of running to the smoke shop to buy his cigarettes. He captured moles and threw them into his yard. Instead of being his little page, his squire. Instead of raking dead leaves from his lawn. Instead of washing his car.

I'd capture moles and I'd toss them into his yard, over the wall.

He tells us this today as though it were his mightiest feat of arms. He couldn't be prouder if he'd bitten Gandhi. From time to time, while still talking, he picks a scale of dead skin from his cheek or forehead with a fingernail.

Mere footsteps away, Beckett was writing the most powerful pages of literature his era would know. It was hard work; it was a kind of suffering. It didn't come freely. Anguish lets nothing pass. Each word must be wrenched from its maw. Beckett is hunched over his table, writing. Sometimes he raises his head. Through the window, he sees a mole flying. Then a second, which, like the first, lands with a heavy thud in his flowerbeds. Or rather no. Beckett has been absorbed in his work for hours. Outside, the day is fading. Beckett raises his head to contemplate his lawn as it turns blue in the dusk. It is a sight that soothes him each night, after writing. But there, stretching out before him, as far as the eye can see, is a devastated terrain of burial mounds, all the day's dead now buried in his yard.

I knew Samuel Beckett well. Sometimes I even tossed as many as twelve consecutive moles into his yard.

Instead of putting himself at his service. Instead of keeping watch over the surrounding silence. Instead of scraping the dirt from his shoes after a long walk. Instead of polishing his walking stick.

Picture Beckett, the handsome face of Beckett, sculpted into the bone: a steep face, with no footholds for viciousness or vulgarity, those clammy expressions that lose their grip and slip right off. Picture the high haughty silhouette of Beckett, the piercing point of his eternally youthful gaze. Think of his books. And now here's this guy telling us about how he applied himself, throughout his childhood, to being the utter bane of his existence.

I'd smoke them out of their molehills. As soon as the frightened moles came out of the ground, I'd capture them. Sometimes

I knocked them out without killing them, with the flat side of a shovel, and sometimes I'd catch them with my father's shrimping net. Then I'd toss them with a steady hand into Beckett's yard, over the shared wall.

There Beckett was, trapped in thought and seeking. And on the other side of the wall, this idiot kid. Beckett seeking at least to know the trap of thought, why its jaw snaps us up so. And carrying this search forth, without rest or respite, and not without success, some of the time. And not keeping that success to himself, no, keeping only the wound and the burn, giving away the healing and the vengeance. Then raising his head and through the window discovering the devastated yard. The moles have destroyed everything with their little pink hands. How unbearably sad! Volcanoes are more considerate of their surroundings.

It was me! I was the weapon that launched them. I was the one who tossed all those moles over the wall that separated our yard from Beckett's.

He's boasting. Even today, it brings him total satisfaction. Then he peels a black scab from his temple with his fingernail. His gaze lingers on every detail of the bodies of his female colleagues at the Lycée Désiré Nisard. His tongue, too pale a pink, passes and passes again, limply, over his cracked dry lips. He lets his fingernails grow out, uses them for things we already know about—though we'd have preferred to remain ignorant. He knew Samuel Beckett. He was a little thumb on the scale of his destiny.

If Beckett took up shovel and spade to repair the damage caused by the moles, it was because of him. Or should we say, more accurately, it was his fault. It was his fault, many times over, that Beckett was forced to interrupt his work. He pushed away the page on which the means to honorably escape the trap of thought, to destroy it or rather make it play in our favor, were coming into focus at last. Beckett went out into his yard. He wandered sadly among the molehills. Maybe he saw another mole fall from the sky, into the grass, and did not kill it. On the other side of the wall, the neighbors' boy shouted shrilly.

It was me!

Who else? Just as stupid today, and bad-hearted, and pleased with himself. We ask around discreetly and find out where he lives. We follow him home. We concoct plans of revenge.

We would have liked to live next door to Beckett. We would have taken care not to breathe too loudly. We'd have sooner died than cough. Our cherry trees would have flung their most beauteous branches over the shared wall. That's much more the kind of relation we would have cultivated with Beckett. There would have been no question of moles whatsoever in our relations with Beckett. We would have settled there, next door to Beckett's house, and been the silent neighbors writers dream of. He might have thought we weren't even home.

Well, I'm telling you about the moles, but I also made a lot of noise. Plus I didn't just toss moles into Beckett's garden, but also slugs, toads, pinecones, rocks. Everything was a projectile. Everything went over the wall. A dead cat, once. That took some finding.

And so he talks and talks, and with a fingernail peels away his scabs, his dead skin. May leprosy carry off the rest!

An Encounter

How simple it is, the face that's never met the fist! The fist distributes the eyes, nose, and mouth on the face. It assigns them the place that will henceforth be theirs. A simple adjustment, but it changes everything. The right eye and the left eye permute. The lips shall be three. And me, asks the nose, where shall I go? Always a surprise.

Before it meets the fist, the face floats. It's fuzzy. The fist focuses the face. There's the face before the fist and the face after the fist. This latter face is the real face, the face revealed, the one to know. The face before the fist is smooth and soft, waiting for the fist. The face before the fist is a rubber face. The fist will give it its shape, fix its traits once and for all. First the fist finds the face's place in space. Then the fist draws the contours of the face. But right after that it puffs, puffs up. It puffs up without exploding, which is what's so surprising.

I had no face. I was facing up to it, miserably. The fist filled in the empty space between my collar and my cap.

The fist finds its place under the brow, with the eye. The fist plants the nose, peremptory, where it pleases. The fist makes space in the mouth for the teeth. Before it met the fist, my nose could only pump air in and out and sniffle.

Now, look out, it's a nose to be reckoned with. It wants the neck all to itself.

A fist. My face. I make the introductions. Then I take my leave.

The fist is like everyone: it loves nothing more than the electrifying touch of a lip. It wants the lip to spread across the sad pallor of the face. It wants the lip, pink and tender, to be everywhere. It swells up the lip all out of proportion. Such is the kiss of the fist, that the whole face is eaten up by the lip pink and tender. The face is swallowed whole by the lip pink and tender. The lip pink and tender covers up the nose, eye, and forehead. The lip pink and tender is the face's eyelid now.

Everything the fist crushes grows back more vigorously. It pushes, but only on springs. It lets Jack pop out of his box. I am exposed. The fist revealed me. I had been hidden behind myself.

He whose nostrils pinched themselves for nothing. He whose eyes squinted for a song. He who turned up his nose at everything. That wasn't me. Here is my real face, on display all over. My eye is a globe, not an almond. My nose has the fat red jowls of a career drinker. My lip has grown so much that all its hems have come undone.

The fist uproots the bridge of the nose and sets it down to span the black eye's Black Sea. The fist tenderizes the face's choice meat, a nice cut. The fist feeds you. Copiously. It fills your mouth with blood: you taste yourself, know yourself. You know the other side of the mask.

The fist receives so little of the face in return. That's why it's often repulsed by the encounter. It has nothing to gain. A waste of time for the fist. When you consider what it gives!

The relief that comes all at once to what was so flatly itself. That new thickness of being. That sudden gain in volume between collar and cap.

The fist is a child's hand. It can only draw little bubble-people. No denying, however, that it has a style all its own. Yes, no more fine-featured face of feline or ferret. The fist has pulverized that pretty little face. And just like that, we no longer even know the meaning of the word *punim.*

The chin is the first to be served by the fist. The fist would feel remiss passing over the chin. The chin reaches out to it so politely. The chin is a part of the route.

Come in, sit down, says the face. And sometimes the fist allows itself to be persuaded. It honors the face with its visit. It doesn't take long to make its mark. The fist sinks into the face. It is in conquered territory. Make yourself at home, says the face. And the fist ensconces itself comfortably in the face's folds.

The fist knows the shortest route to the face. When it's promised to come, it doesn't take three days to make the trip. It sets off and there it is. The fist carefully makes up the face. For this it has a little helper lend a hand. It puts some red on the lips with the eyebrow brush. It puts some blue on the eyelids. Admire the delicate work, the sureness of the stroke.

The fist doesn't want to linger. As soon as it arrives, it's already retreating. But there's no doubt it was here. I have two tongues in my mouth. So it was here. Did you have that snout yesterday? No. So it was here. I went unnoticed. I was invisible to the eyes of the world. Then the fist came and now the crowd parts respectfully when I appear, as at the passage of a king.

The fist was here and now all the fingers are tensed. Look

how puffed up that one is! We'll know when it receives a visit from the fist! A bit of modesty wouldn't do it any harm!

Mirrors don't get used to this face either. They blink. They cloud up. Often they too burst into shards.

But so many faces wander eternally in search of the fist. So many faces look like so many other faces. Regimental faces, faces in the crowd, faces for enumeration and the hecatomb. Faces that haven't met the fist. Faces that don't know the sneer and the wide eyes. Faces that will say Oh! and then Ah! and never anything else. Faces without traces. Faces that have never met the fist.

The fist distinguishes your face from all other faces. Your poor little hazel eye that never attracted a second look, suddenly that's all anyone sees. It shines in its black velvet case like some pure gem. Wish you had two, don't you? But the other one has rolled under a piece of furniture.

The fist never misses its mark. It reaches the face, and the face immediately blossoms. It's springtime. Everything is in bloom. Everything is in flower. What we thought was dead. There is the smile before the fist, which is a frail rowboat. And there is the smile after the fist, which swells up and unfurls like a wave. You smile and all the little boats sink and the beach is engulfed. Maybe some small children even drown. Too bad for those innocent souls.

We thought only the sex organ was capable of turgidity, of budding at the hand's touch. Now aren't you a funny sight: your boxer shorts envy your balaclava! How the fist must have cajoled you! The fist strikes just where it strikes, on the face. The cheeks go magnificently starry. The gums never say no to a bit more scarlet and purple. And the forehead claims there is intelligence coursing through its lumps.

Come back! begs the face. But the fist has too much to do. All those anxious faces waiting. It's asked for all over. It can't do everything; it's only got two hands.

One day I had that good fortune, I who speak to you now. Around a street corner, my face met the fist.

Decalcifies and Disinfects

People speak to me and I don't understand a word. And when I think I understand, I understand badly, I understand wrong, I understand something else. It would be better not to understand anything at all. I have one satisfaction, however: I'm not alone. When I speak, no one understands me either. They don't understand me or they understand me badly, they understand me wrong, they understand something else. It would be better not to understand anything at all, just as I was saying. As I was saying to myself, I mean, because it would obviously be useless to say it to anyone here—I could just as well say the opposite thing and it wouldn't be understood any better. Best to keep it quiet, then. Best to keep quiet, period. And they should do the same: then we'd all stop misunderstanding one another, which would at least be something. But some silences are deceiving too. Is no communication possible?

I am far from the lands where my language is spoken, as you have no doubt understood. Understood, have you? Really? If only you knew how agreeable it is to get on without either gesticulating or botching the English already butchered by the Americans. Which I absolutely refuse to do, in the same way I refuse to polish off the last Mohicans with a Winchester. That informative, utilitarian airport English

93

that accommodates both the Chinese accent and the Uruguayan seems to have been developed for small-scale arms trafficking. I have no business with it, nothing to sell and nothing to buy.

I am far from the lands where my language is spoken and all of a sudden it's like nothing comes out of my mouth but noise. Instead of those well-turned phrases I ordinarily utter without a second thought, nonsensical eructations. Even when I talk to myself I'm not entirely certain I understand. I can guess roughly what I mean, but sometimes I get it wrong. And so it happens sometimes that I act against my own interest, or miss an event I'd planned to attend. If only I were simultaneously progressing in my comprehension of the language spoken here! No such luck. There is no recompense, no justice. What I lose on one side is not restored to me on the other. I must resign myself to the relief of finally joining the rest of the world, of being as incomprehensible to myself as I am to everyone else. But this isn't enough to make me feel the solidarity of a community, one to which I truly belong. The transactions are virtually devoid of emotion.

It's at this moment that I decide to go freshen up in the restroom of this restaurant where I am lunching, alone, on a plate of guinea fowl wattles with raw radishes, which I ordered by pointing to a random line on the indecipherable menu. And as I wash my hands I notice, attached to the plumbing system, a white plastic casing on which I read: DÉTARTRE ET DÉSINFECTE. Yes, you have correctly read these words written in proper French, in excellent French, DECALCIFIES AND DISINFECTS, these intelligible words now etching themselves, clear as day, into my mind, now become lucid, even penetrating, once again.

And in this instant it is my distant country that comes back to me, its fresh odors of foam and gorse and lilac, its streams between stones singing our old *chanson réaliste* repertoire, its little animals of the high grasses, the vole, the shrew, ah! and the snow on its vales, and the sand so fine on its beaches . . . And I tilt my head to drink long drafts of water from the faucet, certain that this plumbing is healthy and sound, that the whole industrial apparatus of my country is seeing to it, our engineers are on the case, actively decalcifying and disinfecting, that the words of my language have not abandoned me in my exile either.

And the delicious water splashing over my face mingles with my tears.

The Rabbit

They make these gadgets nowadays. This one is a slip-cover for a car seat headrest, decorated with an embroidered rabbit's head and topped with two big plush ears. It makes you smile once, maybe.

These objects are taking over, these childish, idiotic, *fun* objects. Gorillas are all bean bags now, full of polystyrene beads. The elephants all serve herbal tea. I defy you to find me a koala without straps or a zipper down its belly.

The necktie has lost none of its paltry gravity for turning into a cartoon. The toe sock doesn't make the quadrumane. The bear's-foot slipper doesn't know how to walk anymore. It crawls. It drags. We live among these gadgets like unhinged elderly children.

This one, in any case, mimics the head of a rabbit and adorns the driver's seat of a little blue car, a trendy model. It's a white slipcover with two round eyes and a black snout embroidered on it. Plus a big stupid smile.

What stand out most, though, undeniably so, are the two ears on the thing. Two big white plush ears, pointy, pinched lengthwise onto a patch of pink cloth that represents the soft mucous membrane. The illusion doesn't claim to be perfect. They want to distract us from the too-human smile, no doubt. Because they remembered the soft mucous membrane, they can permit themselves the ill-chosen smile, so unlike the lover of clover or alfalfa.

A professor of natural sciences couldn't use this slipcover as an anatomical model for his class on lagomorphs, for instance. Real rabbits never smile. Though sometimes a blade of grass or one of their eyelashes tickles them and they flop over on their back. That's like laughing.

They're sweet with each other. Above all, to paraphrase the Latin proverb, rabbit is rabbit to rabbit. Rodents' teeth have better things to do than smile.

The two plush ears must bob a bit when the car is moving, more or less in keeping with how fast it's going, with the surface of the road. At the moment, of course, they're not moving. One is folded back, behind the head; the other is standing up, broken in the middle, point pointing forward, comically. If you like. If you find everything funny.

Why do this? Why surround ourselves eternally with children's playthings? To feel better, we hasten to answer. In the days when we lived among plush animals, however, weren't we scared of everything—darkness, storms, men, dogs? Maybe we'd have been better off seeking the root of our anxieties in this original scenery, peopled with grimacing monsters.

Foam and rubber have flat, gleaming eyes that hang on by a single thread. Foam and rubber take themselves for bears or monkeys, and dust believes it's their fleas. Now there's something more terrifying than the good-humored grizzly bear.

So here's this mossy, plushy, smiling rabbit. It's cute. It's hilarious. It has a sweet-looking face and those funny ears that probably bob when the car is driving on an uneven surface. Just now, of course, they're not moving.

The slipcover is stretched over the headrest, which gives the embroidered rabbit an extremely dilated look. Why the wide face? The real rabbit has the head of a rat, with a long thin snout. It looks nothing like this. Just you try gathering rosemary with that flat muzzle. Go on. Bring me a few sprigs as proof.

In spite of which this rabbit is smiling, and smiling all the more because its face is so wide. Its happy smile stretches across its happy cheeks. Ooh what a nice little bunny-wunny!

We require baby things all around us now: soft things, smooth things, pillowy things. Not only does the crocodile no longer have a lower jaw; its upper jaw is trimmed with supple silks and we take it by the tail to brush our teeth. We fall asleep in the big soft arms of our pandas. The teddy bear is the padded wall of our modern hysteria. We drool all over it.

The salt and pepper shakers are two little sillies who wink and act like herons or ladybugs for our amusement. The egg cup has two legs now, and even though it still has no idea where it comes from it seems to know where it's going. At the bottom of my plate, under a light salad, is an inedible porcelain cow.

And in the smoking shell of the little blue car, the trendy model, smiling stupidly at the men outside who are hacking away at the driver's-side door with electric saws, is this ridiculous rabbit. It rained this morning. The roads were bad. The young lady missed her turn.

Othon Péconnet

For a long time, on the rue Othon Péconnet in Limoges, there was an umbrella merchant. He may still be there today. Even when she was a hundred years old and deeply amnesic, my grandmother remembered it, that umbrella shop on the rue Othon Péconnet. Now, throughout my entire childhood, whenever the rue Othon Péconnet was mentioned in my presence—which was rare but did occur from time to time, particularly when the clouds gathered in the Limousin sky and we found ourselves beneath it—I heard "Othon Péconnet" as though it were a single, strange word, one whose meaning escaped me but whose sound was pleasing, its hard consonants crackling like an onomatopoeia: *otompéconé*.

What might the uses or functions of an otompéconé have been? Was it an object, and if so what kind? A creature, perhaps, but of what species? A country, but where? Finally I dared to ask, though not without trepidation: for all I knew the rue Othon Péconnet was a seamy street in Limoges's red-light district where they bought and sold more than just umbrellas. Could an otompéconé be a kind of brothel? That was the case with the *lupanar,* for instance, a comical term no less liable to elicit the laughter of a pure-hearted child like I was, whose tongue would melt many more sour candies before it ever found its way into a rectum.

But no, nothing of the sort with the otompéconé. Indeed, it was revealed to me to be the first and last name of a man, Othon Péconnet—Péconnet, Othon—who held the office of mayor of Limoges from 1862 to 1867. Seized with passion for my subject, I researched further and discovered that Othon Péconnet was the direct descendant of a royal notary from the fifteenth century, Psaumet Péconnet. The naming of notable Limousins was evidently proof of a minor tradition of familial burlesque, whose brunt was also borne by Psaumet's eldest daughter, Mariote, and his son Narde.

In 1864, a firework spread inopportunely from the sky to the ground and devastated an entire neighborhood of Limoges. Local history records that on this occasion Othon Péconnet proved himself equal to his post, organizing rescue aid, relocating the displaced, and later rehabilitating the neighborhood. But time moved on, and the gratitude soon faded from the hearts of his fellow citizens. Ask a kid from Limoges today who Othon Péconnet is: in the best of cases, he'll point you to the street bearing that name and perhaps add, benevolently, as a drop of rain lands on him, that there's an umbrella shop there. More likely he'll pull his hood over his eyes without answering you and run to take shelter from the storm under a porte cochere. Of Othon himself, such as he is, he will have nothing to tell you.

And more's the pity. It's regrettable that the name Othon Péconnet should have died with the person. The need for Othon Péconnet can be felt today, it seems to me, perhaps even more urgently than ever, and not just for containing fires. Not at all for that reason, in fact, as our modern firefighters have access to faster trucks and stronger hoses than their nineteenth-century counterparts, even water bombers if necessary. No: what we're missing, what we're so cruelly missing, is guys named Othon Péconnet.

We could use some of those, don't you think? At least one. Even just one Othon Péconnet. How much sweeter life would be, how much more bearable, if from time to time we could call to Othon Péconnet in the street. Othon! Hey, Othon, ho! And he'd turn around. He'd walk toward us. With that Othon Péconnet walk. That Othon Péconnet smile on his lips. See how everything changes when you have someone named Othon Péconnet in your life? It's just not the same after that. Something *happens.* What exactly that something is, of course, is impossible to say. Therein lies the mystery of Othon Péconnet. Ineffable, impalpable. An evanescent impression. An emotion.

I've just filed a request with the court clerk of the Republic to legally change my name. I want to give Othon Péconnet another chance—and in so doing, I don't mind telling you, make a fresh start of my life.

Significant Improvements

It was quite sudden. I noted an astonishing improvement in my intelligence. Questions about the human condition in general and my own innermost enigmas alike, questions that had remained obscure to me until now, came clear all at once. All at once, I had gained access to a superior plane of understanding.

And yet I hadn't changed anything in the way I was living my life. I was not reaping *in fine* the fruits of long and patient study. Nor was there anything that might have come from the events of my existence. They say certain ordeals have potent effects on our individual constitutions: that some veil is torn, that intimate revelations appear.

But I had been treated rather sparingly by fate of late, with no great joy to speak of either; it had been a year without griefs and without new beginnings. I could find no specific cause to credit for this sudden profusion of lucidity, of sagacity, of capacity. But it was undeniable: I now grasped that which had once eluded my ken. Endowed with new powers of philosophical penetration, I also pierced through the dense enigma of mathematics. And, in turn, my mastery of this latter science opened to me a metaphysics of the most abstract, the most abstruse nature.

My behavior changed. I now spent most of my days sleeping. Curiously, this lethargy had no detrimental effect on my physical condition. On the contrary, I discovered a new agility in those rare moments when I betook myself to add some action to my life. So I jumped over the retaining wall outside my garden in a single bound. I walked on the ridges of rooftops without fear. I climbed trees and no longer felt the vertigo that once paralyzed me.

But I moved only for the sake of amusement and diversion. Because, once my intellectual faculties increased so dramatically, I no longer had to work for a living. No more daily chores, no more crude subsistence labors. I gave my notice. As though the genius that distinguished me were obvious to everyone, I was exempted from contributing to the works of the community and, as a corollary, from paying taxes.

I am fed. Twice a day at least, a heaping plate is set in front of me. I no longer have to catch or harvest my lunch; if I still hunt from time to time, it's for sport, for my own pleasure, though with more skill and precision than before— and without the aid of my dog, who has become useless and, might I add, quite despondent at my aloofness. He's been rather aggressive toward me ever since. I'm afraid I'm going to have to let him go. I'll give him away, if anyone wants him?

Sensual pleasures no longer resist my desire. The caresses that once fled from me like feral birds now find me of their own accord. Long slender fingers with painted nails scratch my chest. I can, without fear of the slaps that often used to punish such audacities, rub myself against the legs of the prettiest women, even slip under their skirts. They no longer take offense.

Thus the intelligence that was placed upon my forehead like a mark of divine favor affords me plenty of advantages, plenty of attention, plenty of offerings. This makes me all the happier, all the luckier, because intelligence, for all I knew of it before, for what I perhaps possessed of it, seemed to me to be regarded rather poorly: it was abased, ridiculed, scorned. Mine, on the contrary, is the object of a sort of cultish adoration that I enjoy quite naturally—without cynicism, make no mistake, but without shame or remorse either.

I did not come by these rewards illegitimately, in short. The prodigious understanding of beings and things with which I am endowed allows me to conduct myself with greater ease and surefootedness, that's all. And the system that once oppressed me now redounds to my benefit. It plays in my favor.

Eventually I realized that I'm not alone. We are a handful who have received this gift of intelligence. We make up a loose community, one with no society, no rites, no religion, no rules. Nonetheless, we recognize each other immediately. Sometimes the night draws us together. During the day we barely associate. So as not to give ourselves away, we keep our distance. Better to remain discreet. Others would begrudge us. Perhaps they would mistreat us. So we merely squint our eyes. We brush as we pass. And each of us goes his own way.

Then curls up in his basket, on his cushion, and begins almost immediately to purr.

The Pup

That's the one I want.

Dogs: in these cages and these pens are dogs of all sizes, black ones, yellow ones, some so old that the learned man who dares multiply their age by seven will die before he's done calculating; dogs with potbellies, sparse coats, teats flabby and brown, one curtained eyelid, dry noses; there are red ones, white ones, curly-haired or not, with spots or without, dogs of all breeds (and, precariously perched on four legs of unequal length, their thousand paradoxical hybrids); there are wide ones, slim ones, with more or less tail, more or less ear, some looking dreadful, others you'd wipe your feet on, whining with anticipation because you're about to do just that; and then there's this tiny black and white puppy running around all over the place, yapping joyously.

He's the one I want, that little one there.

The speaker, pointing at the animal with a white and blue finger (a bone and a vein), stiff-jointed, slightly crooked, ending in a many-faceted yellow fingernail, is an old woman, or her mummy, or maybe her mother; a very old woman, as though she's already started in on another century, before everyone else, widowed early and often since the age of maturity and whose first husband, perhaps, was the clever wheelwright who first thought to make them round; a scrawny little person dressed in thick gray covered in black, scarf too, despite the heat of this fine summer day; a ruin all in angles and cracks and fissures, the kind preferred by centipedes and lichens. You'd be unsurprised to see moray eels worming out from such a wreck—and indeed there's one now, poking its head out of her astrakhan collar.

Is it housebroken at least?

She's haggling out of habit, out of reflex, but her choice is made. No need to bend down to examine the pup; she's already as stooped as a staircase deliveryman. Ideal silhouette for a veterinarian, really. Could easily castrate a bull calf just as she is. She's wrinkled her forehead. And when she wrinkles her forehead her eyes close halfway, her mouth cracks open just slightly, and you might think she's dying. Which isn't not the case. Death is carrying her away from us as we speak. All will be consumed by this winter at the latest. She'll be laid to rest with her late husbands, amid their ashes, their dust: even in life, that's all they were good for in the house. In the end, they've barely changed at all. Typical. It will all start over as it was before, not that this seems to delight her overmuch.

You swear you don't have any younger ones?

The man from the kennel shakes his head. This is the youngest. Just weaned. A little black and white puppy, cute and very lively, with big round ears that flop comically over his eyes and a wagging nub of a tail. He's playing with a ball. The old woman clings to the fence of his enclosure with her ten fingers and her nose. Has she spent her whole life in those black slippers? Her smile, all out of elasticity, droops down to her ankles. She breathes noisily, especially when inhaling, as though her breath is hauling in earth and stones for her grave. Her breath is more natural as it leaves her. The puppy bounds after his ball: this kind of behavior will have to stop.

I'll take him.

She'll take him! She'll adopt him. He's hers. She'll call him Pom-Pom. He'll be dressed in a plaid jacket in the winter and a raincoat on rainy days. He'll learn to move less, less energetically, to match his pace to the old woman's. In any case, a very short leash will mostly keep him from following his whims. But he'll have a cushion to enjoy. He'll eat leftovers—lucky beast if he likes leeks vinaigrette; she never finishes her whole ramekin. In the afternoon they'll drag themselves across the street to the park. He'll have to obey her, all right. He's hers now. They'll grow old together. Because life's not finished with her, oh no no. What did you think?

Hey now! I've just bought another fifteen years.

The Staircase

What a dim opinion we must have of our own wits to cede to the staircase the responsibility of bringing us up! It's as though we prefer schlepping to soaring, gracefulness be damned. The staircase! What even *is* this useless piece of furniture cluttering up the house with all its open overturned drawers? What was he looking for, the cat burglar who left everything upside down like this? Even the best-kept homestead still has to put up with such disorder. And it's only too easy, alas, to imagine what our guests must think: *Their children are grown and they still don't put away their blocks!*

Like the spine of the diplodocus, the staircase dates from the earliest age of the earth and now belongs with the other fossils in museums of natural history—certainly no longer in our tiny, cramped dwellings, where we'd rather leave some room for the piano, whose teeth are at least more tidily set. And it's impossible to use the staircase without the fear of its upper jaw suddenly clamping down on us with a dry snap and the simultaneous crack of crushed bones. Let us also note that the piano has a mute for a foot—the same foot, by contrast, whose stampede the staircase amplifies beyond proportion: you almost expect to see a herd of bison charging, when in fact it's just the scrawny accountant from the fourth floor coming down with a stealthy step in selvage slippers to peer through the keyhole at Mademoiselle Fifi, the milliner, at her vanity. (Too late, you were there first.)

We can't stand the staircase anymore; we won't stand for the staircase anymore! It still sometimes curls up in a spiral, like a snail bedeviled by a blade of grass, and the sudden constriction almost steals our breath forever. But as a general rule, it presents as a kind of toboggan designed for torment and torture, trimmed with sharp ridges, the better to break our ribs one by one. Steep as an Alp on the ascent, but without the charm of the mountain path, without the miraculous and fortuitous sighting of a chamois or buzzard or larch; at best you'll encounter the concierge, Madame Floursop, whose formidable chest and stomach will flatten you against the wall; at worst it will be your prattling landlord Hector Fang, the most tedious kind of social climber. (The nineteenth-century tone of this text has not escaped my attention, but am I to blame if the staircase leads inexorably to such things, jouncing us along as disagreeably as a carriage on paving stones before the invention of asphalt?)

How do we escape this trap, my friends? How do we put the staircase permanently behind us—or, more accurately, beneath us, like so much vile matter evacuated for good, with repugnance but not remorse? It's quite simple: stay upstairs! Let us not come down, my friends, let us no longer tumble to the bottom, let us never again leave the summits we've attained, let us live on the upper levels and push away with a blow of the heel both the staircase and the temptation of the fall. Let us break that bond that tethers us to the ground, cast away that bridge, and ascend at last to the heights of the eagles and the angels!

The Museum Visit (3)

Modern man is more predictable than the thaw that accompanies the return of mild weather, and it's no great challenge to unravel the mystery of his presence in museums: he's there to slake his thirst for masterpieces, to drink—not without first swirling them around in the glass of his bifocals with a connoisseurly expression on his face—the magenta or vermillion vintages of those artists posterity has consecrated as masters of their art. This is the same inventive mind you'll see walking into a bakery to buy bread, or going to the doctor when afflicted by sickness. Such conformism breaks my heart. Obviously we can expect no more surprises from him than we would from a pear. It's always just going to be a pear. Give him a hat, he'll wear it on his head. Shoes? He'll put them on his feet! And when he's going for extravagance, he'll sport, without fail—wait for it—an extravagant suit.

I care little for the great masters. And so, as with beautiful women, I ignore them, for they already have hundreds of eyes trained on them like leeches. No wonder they're so thin and disenchanted! And the sublime panorama, the majestic vista? I turn my back to them resolutely, refusing to be the subject of such a majesty. Give me the desolate and solitary wasteland, the shadowy recesses of condemnation, arid sands as far as the eye can see.

For what reason, then, can I be seen strolling endlessly through museum galleries? What am I *doing* there? This is the question boring into your skulls like the termite into the roofbeam that holds the firmament aloft. Well then know this: I have come for the minor masters, the unknown, the forgotten. I have come to admire the *Presumptive Portrait of Madame Floursop Attributed to Jules Pinyon After Fido Bazin (or His Atelier),* the chiaroscuros of Anthracite Lenoir, the camp followers of Horace Bonin, the secondary figures of trowelism, the seascapes of Auvergnat Blot, the *Four Thieves* of Hector Ragonit, known as Squinty, the dawnscapes of the belated impressionists, the sole painting by Breughel the Vague Cousin, the busts of Constant Parkinson, the overripe nature scenes of Clémence Poupée, *The Bathed,* a boiling-oil painting by Benjamin Forelock, the juvenile work of Räsel the Elder, curiously kindred to the mature work of Räsel the Younger (whom I also like), the neo-archaism of Burg Stammer (*Communion on the Grass*) and the proto-academicism of Pierre Petitpierre (*The Roman Building Sites*), the renascent decadentism of Flavio Philipo, the series of *Self-Portraits Without Glasses* by Célestin Bourne, *Young Girl with a Round of Gruyère* by the high-society painter Amedeo d'Orfin, *Two Beached Whales* by the abstract miniaturist Lucien van Loope, the vast compositions of the religious and mythological historical painter Henri Maisonneuve (*Saint George Slaying Dragons at Waterloo; The Abduction of las Meninas; The Animals Setting Sail on the Ark for Cytherea*), or even *Lemons and Spring Chickens Under the Sun,* from Anatole Brossard's verdigris period, inauspiciously yellowed by the light that stares down on it through the museum's stained-glass window, each of these masterpieces having been treated with scandalous flippancy by the curators, so that to see them you have to crane your neck and remember to look behind the doors pressed flat against the walls.

Innumerable, nonetheless, are the treasures to which the dumb crowd turns blind eye and cold shoulder. Some of the most remarkable pieces are hiding in private bequests; for instance, the museum in Santonville was forced, in order to take possession of its Renoir, to accept the final wishes of Raoul Trimble and dedicate an entire room to his collection. So while the mob gathers to see a pink girl in a white dress tying a blue ribbon in her blond hair, let's admire the lunar yet earthy landscapes of Saturnine Lancer, the melted-snow landscapes of Flora Moat, the "vanativities" of Petrus Rossignol that depict Virgins breastfeeding crucifixes, and the hunting scenes François Loncle made in a glade on birch bark with beagles' tails and boar blood.

Sometimes a generous widow still gifts the museum the complete works of her late husband, a painter who picked up some prizes once at this or that provincial art fair, and there too I find a thousand occasions for pleasure and ecstasy: didn't this daring, obstinate man encompass unto himself all the artistic revolutions of his century? So rather than tire ourselves out by going to see, one by one, Cézanne, Monet, Gauguin, Matisse, Mondrian, Malevich, Picasso, and Rothko, let us linger before the oeuvre of the singular and prolific Jules-Edouard Torqueboeuf, who magnifies them all consecutively with his vigorous stroke—and let us leave his widow to mourn in an apartment whose bare walls have just been repainted white, then carry on packing her suitcases (she's off to Venice with a gentleman from the neighborhood).

The Gift

She gives him a gift, his stern-faced old wife, and he can't believe it. A gift for the first time in at least twenty years. His sharp-voiced old wife has placed in front of him on the table, next to his plate, wrapped in beautiful paper, carefully trimmed with ribbon, a gift. He hadn't thought of it himself, but he takes stock quickly, makes some calculations, and indeed, today is his birthday. Fifty-nine years, if he's counting correctly. And for the first time in at least twenty his mean-eyed old wife has given him something.

She has placed the little box next to his plate. And yet she's wearing the same nasty grimace as always, perhaps even a bit more pronounced. Is this an attempt at a smile that has failed pitifully due to the atrophy, from infrequent use, of the relevant facial muscles? He feels a stirring of forgotten tenderness. He no longer expected this kind of delicate attention from her. She has surprised him. Is it true, then, that the planet is warming? He suddenly remembers his young wife, her sweet face, her sweet voice, her sweet gaze. How long has it been since he last conjured this erstwhile companion?

He has taken the little box in his hand, a narrow rectangular box, handsomely wrapped. He pulls the ribbon's bow. Then he opens the gift carefully, without tearing the paper.

The old wife watches his reaction, tensed, but her expression remains impenetrable. Her chin trembles a bit, perhaps, barely. Is it emotion that makes her stir like this? He stops mid-movement. He feels he should shake his head, as if to say *Oh you* or *You shouldn't have* or *You never cease to surprise me*—all of it at once, no doubt, or something else, whatever she likes.

It's a pen—a fountain pen, no less, with a gold nib, a mother-of-pearl lining, an old-fashioned reservoir and a screw-on cap. An expensive gift, a luxury brand, a pleasing heft. He doesn't know what to say. He turns the fountain pen awkwardly between his fingers. His eyelashes flutter quickly to hold back his tears. Never would he have thought he could still be moved by a gesture from his dried-up old wife, who over the years has become so sour, so scornful. He sputters some thanks. He kisses her hard forehead. Fifteen years, at least, since his lips last touched that skin.

He turns the fountain pen and turns it again between his fingers, unscrews and rescrews the mother-of-pearl cap. He remembers his writerly aspirations, long ago, his plans, his novel, *Russian Leather,* rejected by all the publishers, restarted a hundred times and finally abandoned. Like the majority of his undertakings, for that matter, when he thinks about it. It's so hard to see things through. Life is always just ahead and then one fine day it's entirely behind you, right there with that of your ancestors. The mother-of-pearl cap is encircled by a golden ring and glints of reflected light play on it, like a wedding band on brighter days.

And this is what his marriage has become: all spoiled, deteriorated, corrupted, in this sad kitchen, on this sagging sofa, in this shabby apartment. All come to nothing. There was a son, now far away. The body has worn itself out by dint of monotonous work, and will soon be retired anyway. He likes to say he occupies an intermediate position in the chain of command, of orders made and orders executed, but in reality if the hierarchy grows heavier with his weight, it's felt only by an infinitesimal number of subaltern employees, temporary or seasonal, while he has the whole pyramid bearing down on his back.

The elegant fountain pen seems out of place in his hand, this hand he deplores for its ineptitude, its indecision, its awkwardness, its sterility, its inertia. What good did it ever do, really? Did this hand ever make anything beautiful? Did it alter the course of things even a little bit? His existence is a somber failure, a shipwreck, when he thinks about it. Nothing to justify it. Fifty-nine years of time wasted, of days given over to night. He hunches forward a bit more in his chair. He unscrews the mother-of-pearl cap and in a single motion plunges the gold-flaked nib into his throat while his old wife peers at him, her little eyes hard and shining.

The Pan

So obviously the frying pan, when it comes to frying things, is not completely useless. But still, no one but a certain caliber of crazy person devotes his or her entire life to frying foodstuffs in a pan: not even frying professionals, artisans of French fries or fritters or frittatas. Sometimes, yes, and sometimes even the next day as well, we'll fry a thing, but not *all the time,* nobody fries all the time, not from dusk until dawn. And what happens to the frying pan when we stop frying whatever food we were frying? It remains a frying pan! A frying pan, imperturbably a frying pan, as though we were about to go on frying and indeed do nothing but fry, never stop frying again! Wouldn't you say that's just a little bit *cocky?* When we stop frying, couldn't the frying pan follow suit and stop offering us, with laughable tenacity and pretension, its frying services? Couldn't it modestly blend into the background, or just go do something else?

Guess what! Nope. It never leaves its comfort zone, its niche, as though it would find it demeaning to do anything besides fry. I blame my regular tennis losses to Roger Federer on its total inability to adapt to the game and become a serviceable racket. Once it even fried the ball like an egg! The umpire awarded Federer the point, which perhaps I could have contested: was this not, after all, a compelling variation on the drop shot? The matter wasn't discussed, and I didn't bother registering a complaint; it would have been my only point in the match anyway.

The frying pan's incompetence is all but total regarding anything that isn't frying. If it's a lamentable racket, is it any better as a paddle with which to sail up a river? Absolutely not: as I'm sure will surprise no one at this point in my demonstration, all it wants to do is fry the bleaks and minnows it meets in the water. Even when submerged, as far as possible from its little butane flame, it still has no other notion in its flat head! And the frogs are certainly quick to keep their legs away from such a specious lily pad.

So I dock on the grassy bank, depressed, frying pan in hand. Will it deign to take part, for a few moments at least, since I clearly have nothing to fry, in the innocent pastime of catching butterflies? Oh, naughty net! Oh, the carnage! How it smushes the gentle lepidopteran, and the flower it was perched on! What a blow for entomology. What a collection of glittering dust! The frying pan obstinately refuses to do any job but its own. No versatility, no flexibility: it's a soundless banjo, a bladeless shovel, an excessively blunt sex toy, a warped unicycle, a flavorless lollipop, an opaque mirror. We can't get anything else out of it. Just frying.

What's to be done? I ask you once more, friends, what is to be done if we don't wish to perish from despair in this hostile world? Stop frying! Let us deprive the frying pan of its sole raison d'être. Let it finally become that useless object it's so good at being in every other circumstance. Let us make it the idiotic emblem of our resignation to contingency, to senselessness—and then go for a swim in the gentle waves, with fingerlings wriggling all around us, delivered once and for all from fear of the future.

Works

He is signing, for a handful of readers as old as he is, the single volume—solitary but thick and small-printed—of his complete works. Too small-printed for his tired eyes and for those of his handful of readers as old as he is. They could have considered this. It's a solid volume all the same, bound in whole cloth, sea green, with a portrait of the old writer in yellow on a vignette centered underneath the title —WORKS—a woodcut by that painter he once frequented, who is long dead and even longer forgotten.

WORKS. It's nonetheless a pleasure to feel it under his hand, his frail hand that weighs no more now than a leaf. Under this frail hand there is the solid volume. At least two thousand pages inside, each of which had to be written. And it's small-printed. The writer caresses the solid volume. Good and sturdy. No one shall take it from him.

His fingers slide over the hardcover's spine, lingering on a corner that resists under the pressure of the index and middle fingers, that doesn't yield. The old writer smiles with a certain fatuity. It's hard, he seems to be saying. He would be making the same face if he'd invested in brick and mortar. His hand is light, dry, porous, blue, gray, violet, depending on the light. Laid flat on the volume now, like a foot on the flank of a vanquished beast. It wrote all of this. Not a word inside that it didn't trace out itself. And there are plenty of words.

Before the seated old writer, a triple stack of these solid volumes. Sometimes he takes one in both hands. Yes, here at last is his left hand called to the task, required by this work to which it contributed nothing, or precious little. But the right by itself isn't anything anymore. No longer firm enough to even open its own handiwork. It remembers its sister, now that it needs her. The sister bears no resentment for having been so long neglected. Scorned, even, one might say. She rushes to her sister's aid.

WORKS. The writer's mouth smiles proudly, but his gaze is perplexed. A glassy gaze, misted up. It seems less concerned by the solid volume than the mouth and the hand do.

From time to time an old lady, hesitant, blushing, adolescent, asks the writer for an inscription. He unscrews the cap of his fountain pen and writes a few additional words, for her, on the flyleaf, a few more words still, illegible, incomprehensible, full of wit. Then he signs them, as though with a sword. Then the trusty bookseller offers the sweet old lady a little bag.

The writer no longer looks much like the portrait on the cover. But it's the old man he's become who is unrecognizable, in whom he seems to not quite believe. The solid volume has more reality, more future, than this meager character who is not, to all evidence, long for this world. This is what he has done with his life. It's all in here. From the beginning, almost, to the end, almost. Almost all of it.

Nor is it guaranteed to everyone to be able to hold between his hands in this way the sum of his labors, in a single compact block. WORKS. We generally take the writer's activity to be quite abstract; is this not concrete? Feel its weight, feel it. I have lived, says the writer. It's all here. And he pats the solid volume with his hollow hand. Your turn now. Show your worth.

Sometimes it's another old man who shows up for an inscription, often the talkative type, looking to establish a kind of complicity with the author. Often the type who is nostalgic for the old ways, the old manners. You, at least, you know how to write. Whereas today.

There is an amusing contrast between the writer's fragility, his extreme fatigue, his debility, and the sharp rectangularity of his volume. WORKS, bound in whole cloth stretched and glued onto the rigid cardboard of the cover, whereas the writer: old skin, the cardboard underneath rather damaged too. All the writer's youth, all his vigor, we know where they've wound up. He caresses the solid volume. He believes he possesses them still. Does it occur to him, though, that he no longer has the strength even to destroy it, this solid volume? He'd lose to it in an arm-wrestling match. He put all his muscle into it. Even if he turned into an eraser he'd be powerless against it now.

Now, we would be wrong to believe the volume is his tomb. It's worse than that. He is alive inside of it. He will not leave it except to die. For as long as the solid volume exists—it is hardbacked, brocaded, bound to last—the writer will be its prisoner, kept cruelly alive but suffering a thousand deaths: self-unsatisfaction, the incomprehension of others, indifference, and insult are the first four. Oblivion, finally, will be the last.

Here is the old writer trapped like a rat inside the solid volume of his complete works. Like a rat? No. Like a rat, surely not: on the contrary. The solid volume is cheese for the rat.

Elusive

I was about to step out.

With an unthinking motion—executed so many times that my arm knew just what it had to do—I unhooked my hat from the peg on which it was hanging and put it on my head.

Except that no, in point of fact, I didn't put it on my head. Just as my hand—which was thus holding the hat by the brim—was about to place it there, my head suddenly bowed down to my right shoulder and the hat met nothing but air.

Missed!

I'm not a man to give up so easily. I had planned to step out, and I don't step out without my hat. I tried again, aiming a little more to the right to anticipate a possible dodge. This time my head dove forward and my hat landed on the nape of my neck.

Missed it!

How do you like that!

Ordinarily this was a mere formality, putting my hat on to step out. I would take it by the brim and in the same motion place it—or better yet pull it down tightly—onto my cranium, over which its hollow cavity fit perfectly. It was all a matter of reflex, of habit; I didn't have to be conscious of what I was doing. Oftentimes I even thought about other things while I put my hat on.

But today it was precisely my consciousness that put its foot down. It was none too pleased to be so systematically shut out of the procedure, treated in this particular case as useless, even unwelcome. It wanted to direct the maneuver, just as it directed the conduct of my affairs—to remain in control of my body, to be responsible for my person at every moment, down to the most insignificant gestures. It was demonstrating its power: I was nothing without it; without it I amounted to nothing, I would try and try, in vain, in void.

Again I tried to take it by surprise. I took my hat in my left hand and brought it down briskly, over and over, describing stranger and stranger motions, infinite curlicues in the air, wild arabesques, feinting suddenly to put it on and then moving away at the last second to change the spot where it would land: each time, my head, tipping forward or back, lolling on one shoulder or the other, managed to avoid the hat, as though it could predict my ruses and designs.

Missed it! Missed again!

Little by little, however, my frustration gave way to a certain satisfaction. I wasn't so easy to catch, to mislead, all told. Never where you expect him, the old boy: still unpredictable at over fifty, elusive, resistant to routine, fiercely independent, that's what I was, and all at once I took my head's side against my hat. My entire being clamored now for this freedom. I contorted, I jiggled, I wriggled. Then, as the hat was once again arming its gesture, I seized the moment and dove under the table. My wrist banged the table's edge, my fingers released the brim, and I rushed out and slammed the door behind me.

Wham!

The wind caressed my forehead, tousled my hair. I was a man free amid the immensity of the world.

Now there was just the intolerable hindrance of these pants.

In a single bound, I tore them away.

The Soup

I forgot to turn off the burner under the soup. I scraped the carrots, peeled the potatoes, the zucchini, the turnip, the fennel, I did all of that, then I cut those vegetables into pieces, I rinsed them in the strainer, which I then emptied into the pot of salted water, I added a bouillon cube, I lit the gas, I remember the blue flames quite well, the orangey corolla around the burner, so yes, I started the soup, after which I got on with my business and left the house.

Without turning off the burner under the soup, that is—I have no memory of having turned off the burner under the soup. I close my eyes to play back the images, all the action starting with the scissors struggling through the nylon mesh of the potato bag, the fruitless search through every drawer for the peeler. At the end of the film I was supposed to turn off the flame underneath the pot—that was the logical and expected denouement to which this whole dramaturgy was leading; a bit simplistic a resolution, perhaps, but one I carried out with sincerity and panache. Me, turning off the burner under the soup before leaving the house. That's what should have happened. That evening, for the second episode, I would blend the cooked vegetables and reheat the potage—because really, to be precise, it would be more of a potage than a soup, I say soup out of laziness, a lexical convenience. That's not what's important right now.

There was to be a third episode, if the first two were successful, in which I drank my soup. It would not be unfair, I think, in such circumstances, to call it a trilogy. That's not the issue. I left the house two hours ago, and it's impossible for me to get home for another two hours . . . for four hours, then, the fire will heat the pot. All the water will evaporate—that's probably done by now. Then the vegetables will blacken, shrivel, and form a dry crust permanently fused to the metal through an exchange of molecules, a chemical amalgamation, and that's the end of my soup. The ebonite handle of the pot will melt from the heat. The whole apartment will stink for the rest of my life. Not that my death will fix anything.

Is there a risk of explosion? There isn't, right? But drops of ebonite will drip onto the kitchen floor, the linoleum will catch fire, the flames will start to spread everywhere, making themselves at home like mice in the baseboard, cats behind the curtains, owls in the eaves. Everything will burn: my furniture, my carpets, my paintings, my wardrobe which won't ward off anything at all, my books, my archives, my precious manuscripts, and on top of it all I don't even *like* soup, it's disgusting, I have to force myself to choke it down every time! It's healthy, they say. Full of vitamins. What a joke! This soup is going to ruin my life, send my life up in smoke. Eat your soup, they say, they drill it into us, finish your soup, have some more soup . . .

Eat your soup, they've been repeating ever since I was little—and why? So I would grow. Well, the flames will have certainly taken note. How high they must be by now! And soup won't be enough to satiate them. Now they'll need solids, something hearty, something robust, no doubt they've already begun devouring the building, the fire spreading bit by bit through the entire neighborhood. Not only is my soup ruined, but now the occupants of the upper floors are diving from their windows, smoke is asphyxiating babies in their cribs and the bedridden in their beds. Ashes float through the city, landing on lawns and public gardens, in schoolyards, obscuring the view from our windows, whitening our hair, never again will we be carefree, never again will we laugh, no more will we ever know such a thing as joy.

Then I got home. I had not in fact forgotten to turn off the burner under the soup. Ah! Good god damn it all, now I have to drink it!

Acknowledgments

The translator is grateful to the author for his good-natured explanations of certain passages, to Nicolas Richard for helping untangle innumerable intricacies of wordplay (and pointing out several others, to the translator's occasional exasperation), and to Daniel Medin, without whose dedication, stewardship, and finely tuned ear and eye this book would not exist.

The editors extend their thanks to Abbie Storch, John Donatich, Susan Laity, and the rest of the team at Yale University Press, and to Taylor Davis-Van Atta, founding editor of *Music & Literature,* for his support of various English-language Chevillard projects, not least the extensive dossier in Issue 8.

Credits

The credits page constitutes a continuation of the copyright page.

FROM *SCALPS* (2004)

"Pascale Frémondière et Sylvie Masson" (Pascale Frémondière and
     Sylvie Masson)
"Faldoni" (Faldoni)
"Les taupes" (Moles)
"Une rencontre" (An Encounter)
"Le lapin" (The Rabbit)
"Œuvres" (Works)

FROM *COMMENTAIRE AUTORISÉ*
SUR L'ÉTAT DE SQUELETTE (2007)

"Le clavecin" (The Harpsichord)
"Le chiot" (The Pup)
"Le cadeau" (The Gift)

FROM *PÉLOPONNÈSE* (2013)

"Autofiction" (Autofiction)
"La visite au musée" (The Museum Visit)
"Les pierres" (Stones)

"Histoire de la guerre du Péloponnèse" (History of the
    Peloponnesian War)

"Le ciel" (The Sky)

"Vivons cachés dans l'eau limpide" (To Live Hidden in Clear Water)

"La porte" (The Door)

"La visite au musée (2)" (The Museum Visit [2])

"Le froid" (The Cold)

"L'escalier" (The Staircase)

"La visite au musée (3)" (The Museum Visit [3])

"La poêle" (The Pan)

FROM *DÉTARTRE ET DÉSINFECTE* (2017)

"Le guide" (The Guide)

"La chaise" (The Chair)

"Le bonnet de Hegel" (Hegel's Cap)

"Le certificat" (The Certificate)

"Pierre et le loup" (Peter and the Wolf)

"Rapport parlementaire" (Parliamentary Report)

"Un succès inespéré" (An Overwhelming Success)

"Exécration" (Execration)

"Détartre et désinfecte" (Decalcifies and Disinfects)

"Othon Péconnet" (Othon Péconnet)

"Nets progrès" (Significant Improvements)

"Insaisissable" (Elusive)

"La soupe" (The Soup)

ÉRIC CHEVILLARD was born in 1964 in La Roche-sur-Yon. He published his first novel, *Mourir m'enrhume,* in 1987; he has since published some twenty-one novels, short fiction, a long series of book reviews in the newspaper *Le Monde,* and a daily blog (*L'autofictif*). His work has been translated into eleven languages worldwide; seven of his novels have appeared in English, notably *The Crab Nebula, On the Ceiling,* and *The Valiant Little Tailor* (trans. Jordan Stump), *Palafox* (trans. Wyatt Mason), *Prehistoric Times* (trans. Alyson Waters), and *The Posthumous Works of Thomas Pilaster* (trans. Chris Clarke). He was awarded the Prix Fénéon for his novel *La nébuleuse du crabe,* the Prix Wepler for *Le vaillant petit tailleur,* and in 2014 the Prix Alexandre Vialatte, a prize intended to acknowledge writing of exceptional elegance and wit, for the entirety of his work.

DANIEL LEVIN BECKER is the author of *Many Subtle Channels* and *What's Good* and the translator of books by, most recently, Jakuta Alikavazovic and Laurent Mauvignier.

DANIEL MEDIN is professor of comparative literature at the American University of Paris and a director of its Center for Writers and Translators.